MW01172133

Ragna the Dragon Warrior
A Time of Dragons II

by
Cynthia Vespia

RAYNA THE DRAGON WARRIOR

A Time of Dragons Volume II

Copyright © 2023 Cynthia Vespia

All rights reserved.

ISBN: 978-1-7376927-4-4

This book is a work of fiction. While references may be made to actual places or events, the names, characters, incidents, and locations within are from the author's imagination and are not a resemblance to actual living or dead persons, businesses, or events. Any similarity is coincidental.

This book is licensed to the original purchaser only. Duplication or distribution via any means is illegal and a violation of International Copyright Law, subject to criminal prosecution and upon conviction, fines and/or imprisonment. No part of this book can be shared or reproduced without the express permission of the publisher.

Cover Image: ID 198736369 ©Refluo I Dreamstime.com
Back Cover Image: ElixorDesigns on Etsy
Map Design by: AEKCreates on Etsy
Additional Cover Edits: Original Cyn Content

She was once a slayer of mighty dragons,
Now a defender of their kind.

Rayna's vow to protect the last dragon on Atharia has been beset by danger. In all her years of hunting dragons never did she expect her best traveling companion to become one. But with a bounty of blood on their heads that bond will be tested.

Now, as they continue the journey towards the Isle of Dragons, Rayna is challenged by mercenaries, monsters, and a mysterious figure who follows wherever they go. Will the odds become too great or will Rayna rise up as the dragon warrior to quell the evil armies that seek to destroy her?

A beautiful, violent story about revenge and redemption. Rayna the Dragon Warrior continues the exciting fantasy adventure series A Time of Dragons.

CHAPTERS

A Time of Dragons Series

Rise of the Dragonslayer (*prequel*)
Rayna the Dragonslayer - book 1
Rayna the Dragon Warrior - book 2
Rayna the Dragon Defender - book 3

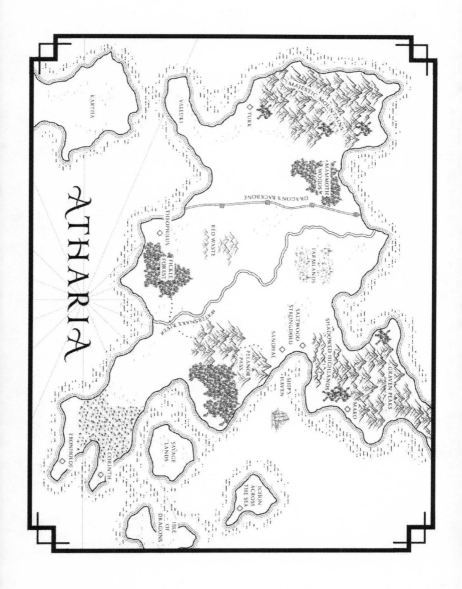

I
First Flame

As a slayer of dragons, Rayna counted only upon her skill and speed to win the day. That she was a woman in body seemed less important than her prowess with a sword. Her mindset changed as a pack of heavily armed mercenaries chased her down.

Being the number one threat to the King of Atharia, a heavy bounty lay on her head. That fee doubled for any man in the land who could abscond with the precious cargo Rayna traveled with.

The words on the bounty scroll were ambiguous. If any knew that Rayna carried a small dragon with her there would no doubt be more would-be hunters on her trail. Entire towns would empty at her passing just to catch a glimpse of Ryu the red dragon.

Having the notorious group the Righteous Wardens galloping up behind her was trouble enough. Their leader, Coraise Kennethgorian, lusted for more than just the massive bounty or even the small dragon Ryu. Coraise wanted Rayna for himself.

She sensed his desires the first time they tangled only to be rescued by a man who bedded then double-crossed her. Since then, Rayna made it a point of not getting into bed with strange men by choice or by force. Coraise had other ideas.

Rayna managed to steal a swift horse from a small farm on the way to taking Ryu towards freedom. It gave Rayna a chance to rest her feet from an arduous journey. But a bit of bad luck brought her right across the path of Coraise and his men.

As Rayna routed towards Valeuki, Coraise and the others were heading away from the city. Rayna almost brought her horse headlong into the pack of them. Too late did she recognize his square jaw and long, dark mane of hair. He was handsome enough but Rayna knew that under his striking features lay a special type of malice reserved for women.

She pulled back on the reins of her horse causing it to rear and whinny. The commotion caught Coraise's attention and when he saw it was Rayna his face broadened with a disgusting grin. Rayna turned the horse ready to gallop all the way back to where she'd left

a trio of human-wolf hybrids dead on the battlefield.
Anything to get as far from the Righteous Wardens as
she could.

It seemed Coraise hired new men to replace the last
that fell by Rayna's broadsword. The massive weapon
she called Bhrytbyrn sat in its cradle on the horse's
saddle. Rayna would need to stop in mid-gallop to
retrieve her sword. But once she had it in hand, her
special connection to the blade would light it up in flame.

Looking over her shoulder, she debated taking the
chance. The Righteous Wardens grew close enough to
make out their scowled faces and missing teeth. If Rayna
stopped now they would all crash into each other.
Thrown from her saddle any number of things could
happen that would not favor a victory. So, she pressed
the horse into a faster gallop.

The chase seemed endless. Many times Rayna tried to
thwart their pursuit by moving in and out of dense
forests. She maneuvered her horse with spectacular
precision around large pine trees. Her hope that the
erratic path would knock a few of the mercenaries off
balance proved pointless. They remained in the chase
without the trees being any hindrance.

Rayna's horse began to tire and her own legs ached
from the rough ride. Soon she would have to stop and
face the men head on. If she fell to this pack of fools the
embarrassment would hurt more than anything Coraise

had in mind for her. Worse still, Ryu would be taken and all would be lost for his kind. But the little dragon decided his own fate.

As the Righteous Wardens inched closer to Rayna, one of them reached out and caught her cloak. He yanked it free from her shoulders to reveal Ryu in his papoose at her back. At first, the mercenary gasped in delight. Then his joy turned to screams of terror.

From her vantage point, Rayna couldn't see the encounter but she knew what happened to the man. The warmth across her shoulders and the chaos of scared, stumbling horses told the tale.

Feeling threatened, Ryu reacted to the mercenary's advances. He levied his first dragon flame directly into the man's face and continued spitting fireballs at the rest of the pack. His attacks weren't the engulfing spread of fire that grown dragons held. But he'd grown enough in such a short time that his flame still did damage one didn't walk away from.

With Ryu defending their back, it gave Rayna a chance to break away from the pack. She put enough distance between herself and the Righteous Wardens to make her feel at ease. Still, she kept a steady pace until she knew she had lost them.

On the crest of a hill in the distance stood Coraise. The sun was at his back silhouetting his tall frame as he watched on. Rayna kept her eyes on him to prepare for

4

his advance. But he would not engage the fight this day. He pointed the tip of his sword towards her to signify they'd meet again, then turned the other way.

Someone the likes of Coraise Kennethgorian wouldn't stop coming after her until one of them was dead. To him it was a sport to hunt down the once mighty dragonslayer. For Rayna, it was life or death not only for her but Ryu as well.

2
Warriors & Dragons

T rying to elude the Righteous Wardens pushed Rayna far off her path. She wound up turned around and miles from any locations she recognized. Ryu fidgeted at her back making loud grunts to vocalize his aggravation. After the scare he'd had she couldn't blame him.

"You did well," she told him. "Hold on just awhile longer."

The chase made them all anxious. Even the horse seemed shaken. More than once he disregarded Rayna's command and she had to forcibly move him back onto the path. Rayna herself felt a trickle of exhaustion come over her as the adrenaline wore down. The elevated response to an impending attack used to enthrall her. Now, she had too much to lose.

Not only did she make a promise to bring Ryu to the

elusive Isle of Dragons, but she had a score to settle as well. Somewhere in the world sat a witch who Rayna owed a debt. She was not about to fall before serving that sentence out.

Lost in a part of the world she usually didn't venture, Rayna circled her horse a few times before moving on. She couldn't return to her old haunts with a bounty on her head. After weighing her options she decided to take a route that looked well-traveled. The dirt showed wear from both hooves and wagon wheels. Branches from bushes and trees had been cut back to allow for cleaner travel.

Not having a thicket growing over the path made it safer from thieves as well. Back when she ran with her adopted brothers in the Forsaken Force, they used the foliage to disguise their intent. It served them well for many years.

Most times Rayna would've preferred the lesser traveled roads. She knew how to spot trouble along the way and how to stay clear of it. But following those paths made her less conspicuous. Even when her name carried fame she preferred the anonymity. Now, with the hefty bounty on her head, Rayna could better avoid detection by seeking the road less traveled.

However, time was of the essence. Her dragon, and her own stomach, demanded sustenance before continuing on their quest. Taking the well-worn path would lead her to a town or city where they could find food and shelter for the night. If nothing else, she may be able to find a farmhouse at the end of the long-winding path. A farmhouse would be preferred. She'd swayed a farmer or two in her day, she could do it again.

Moving in a slow trot, Rayna kept shifting her head to mark the area with her good eye. The wicked one remained hidden beneath a crude, leather patch. Though it sat docile for the moment, the pull of its demands had grown recently. Rayna often wound up with a tremendous headache when she didn't give in to the wants of her dragoneye. One more little gift the witch Nadiuska cursed her with.

Ryu had calmed down but he still did not rest. Rayna felt at ease with him watching her back. Each time he stretched his wings it felt like an extension of herself. It also made her start to question their arrangement. She was meant to be his guardian, but it seemed now they both shared a mutual bond of protection. In all her years of hunting dragons never did Rayna expect her best traveling companion to be one.

As they moved further down the path, Rayna began to get her bearings. She could see from the dark coloring of the earth and the fullness of the leaves that they found their way back towards Valeuki. It was a colorful city known for its spices and wines. The road leading into it was dotted with small clusters of towns. Each of them had been built off the backs of slaves.

Rayna didn't travel to Valeuki often; she couldn't stand the smell of it. When she did find herself in the area she was too drunk to care about the tales being told. Of those Rayna could recall she reflected on the stories of D'zdario Dizdar. A fierce and fearsome pirate who made a great deal of profit in human trafficking.

Not having any use for neither slaves nor ships, Rayna didn't concern herself with such stories. Since tangling with the royals who currently sat on the throne she'd become wary of all manner of mercenary. King Falkon and his family were sea-faring people before invading Atharia and claiming Saltwood Stronghold. It made Rayna wonder if they ever dealt with Dizdar. Rotten scum, the lot of them. They'd sooner slit your throat for a single coin than offer any type of mercy.

Some thought that way about Rayna as well. So, when King Falkon spun his stories about how she'd murdered his father, and his lead council Valerios, the people believed the lies. Even now as she walked her horse past the towns she felt heavy stares on her. These were simple folk, not known for fighting. But given the chance they would tear Rayna from the saddle and beat her senseless.

Though they may be misguided in their judgement, she did not want to kill innocents. Slowly, she slipped a woven blanket over her shoulders and tucked away her blonde hair beneath. The blanket cascaded down over

Ryu and he shrugged it back enough to stick out his snout. He remained vigilant with his watch as Rayna edged her way closer to Valeuki.

3
The Bloodline

Nadiuska stared down from the dais watching the servant girls from her new throne. It was a custom showpiece made of dark mahogany. The wood had been smoothed and polished into sharp peaks and stunning edges. Supple pillows had been wrapped in soft leather and stitched into the seat and backrest.

The throne was yet another gift commissioned by her new husband the king. Whatever Nadiuska desired, he delivered. At first, she started with small requests. But slowly she increased her wants until finally the entire castle was dressed the way Nadiuska wanted it to be: fit for a queen.

All she had to do was keep King Falkon under her spell and he would provide like a puppy needy for affection. Her Daughters of Chaos kept him distracted while Nadiuska transformed the kingdom into her own. But there was one thing Nadiuska desired more than all else and King Falkon consistently failed to deliver it.

The girl and her dragon still roamed free somewhere on Atharia. Nadiuska had lost track of her after Rayna butchered her guard dogs. The Night Howlers were some of Nadiuska's most loyal pets. Now she needed to procure new ones.

She stared over the staff working throughout the halls and determined their worth. One-by-one she dismissed them as useless. Too skinny, too fat, too stupid. None of them carried the killer instinct she needed to complete her plans. Even King Falkon, who showed such promise early on with his malicious intent, grew soft as a pig's belly. For now it seemed Nadiuska could only rely on herself and her daughters.

Setting her chin atop clenched fists she leaned forwards in her throne and began a chant. The whispers were masked by the cascade of her dark hair. It fell over her shoulders and covered her like a cloak. She needed no outside distractions for her communion to work.

Slowly she turned within herself until she felt her spirit lift and begin searching the lands. Fits of images came to her but only in bits and pieces, nothing solid. Then for a moment she saw clearly. The girl's face shone in a wash basin. As Rayna cleansed she relieved the damned eyepatch allowing Nadiuska to see freely once again.

The connection grew much weaker through time and

Rayna's stubbornness. If Nadiuska had known the strength of the girl's resolve she would've chosen a different champion so many years before. Now, even with the fresh blood of a dragon coursing through her veins, her power proved too weak to take control.

As Nadiuska intruded on her thoughts, Rayna pushed her out. The witch would keep trying until she had her puppet back. But then, over the girl's shoulder the red dragon popped up. Though his eyes looked at Rayna he saw only Nadiuska. She felt his hard stare full of hate and it made her smile. Then he snapped his jaws at her and it caused Nadiuska to jump back, effectively breaking the connection.

She leapt in such a way that the servant girls came running to her aide. The witch waved them all off with a shaky hand. The dragon felt her presence and interfered. He would not allow her to connect with Rayna again.

The dragon doubled in size and wit. He was a beautiful specimen and his blood would power her for countless ages. Now, more than ever, Nadiuska needed to find their location.

Before the servant girls exited the great hall she called them back. The older one almost fell over her long skirt as she rushed to Nadiuska's side. The younger two were timid in their approach with heads down and eyes averted. All of them feared their new queen...as it should be.

"Gather the king," Nadiuska told them. "I should like to speak with my new husband at once."

The three servants nodded and hurried off in different directions to find King Falkon. One didn't need a seer to know the odious king was on top of a slave girl somewhere. If he spent half as much time ruling as he did fornicating then perhaps seizing his kingdom wouldn't have been so easy. But then, that is why Nadiuska picked the Fourspire clan so long ago. Their arrogance clashed with their wits leaving them vulnerable to deception and easy to overthrow.

But before Nadiuska positioned herself as high ruler alone on the throne she would use King Falkon's resources. They had spent too much time toying with Rayna. Now that Nadiuska had seen the dragon offspring for herself she would stop at nothing to capture him. If that meant killing the girl, so be it.

4
Killer Instinct

Having Ryu gnash his teeth towards her face startled Rayna enough to make her fall back. She took a spill to the ground which brought unwanted attention from the people of Valeuki. It was a welcome relief when they began laughing at her. Better to be embarrassed than attacked.

Ryu remained perched on the edge of the horse trough where Rayna stopped to wash her face. He watched her every move as though assessing an enemy. Slowly, so as not to startle him, Rayna got back to her feet. He stretched out his wings and parted his mouth to expose his jagged teeth. Animal bites were nothing new to her flesh. Rayna was more concerned with the fireballs he could spew from his throat. She dusted herself off, replaced her hood and the eyepatch. Ryu seemed to soften then. He gave her a chirp then stuck his snout in the water to fetch a drink.

"Is that your way of apologizing?" Rayna asked, still wary of her companion's sudden temper.

Dragons and humans were not meant to co-exist. She'd been foolish to think that enough shared time together bonded them in some way. Ryu was a dragon and dragon's weren't pets. Worse still, Rayna wondered if he could smell the proverbial blood on her hands. In time he'd learn of her deadly past with his kin and then the dragon jaws would come for her again.

Reaching for Ryu to set him once again upon her back she noticed her hands shaking. Flexing her fingers a few times calmed her enough to proceed. The initial shock wore off but she still felt uneasy. It wasn't anything new to have a dragon go for her head. Except in her hunting days she expected the attack and was ready for it.

Something set Ryu off and she needed to find out what that was. First, they needed to feast. Perhaps with his hunger settled her dragon companion would calm down.

Ryu settled at her back once again and Rayna dared to caress his nose. He gave her a hum of approval as though he didn't just try to tear her face off.

"Maybe you're just hungry," Rayna lamented. "Let's find you some food so you don't go for my flesh again."

Whether the townspeople saw the dragon or not they didn't let on. Perhaps the presence of a dragon in their town wasn't any stranger than the usual happenings in

Valeuki. Still, Rayna tried to keep Ryu out of sight as she entered the local eatery.

Valeuki hadn't changed much since the last time Rayna traveled there. It still stank of exotic spices and sex, neither of which appealed to Rayna's ravenous stomach. Their local pub remained a display in color and debauchery. The owners, a pair of gypsies by their own acknowledgement, decorated with a flair that matched their unique personalities.

Tapestries hung from the walls with each telling a different story. They depicted the Source Gods fornicating with each other. Once the God of Wind, Goddess of Earth, God of Fire and Goddess of the Sea came together they spawned the creation of the world...or so the story went. If that were the way of things it was no wonder everyone on Atharia and beyond were touched in the head.

Rayna took a table at the back of the room. She preferred having such a vantage point. It allowed her to keep watch on all angles. More than once, a would-be-attacker tried to get the jump on her and she thwarted it with a quick cut of her sword. Now with Ryu beside her, and the bounty on their heads, Rayna needed to be extra vigilant.

Her watchful eye and situational awareness favored her immediately. The moment she sat down a strange woman began marking her movements. From the look of her, the young woman wasn't from Atharia.

Long, dark hair trailed to her mid-back in a thick braid. She wore a flowing green tunic to her knees that was tied off with a wide emerald sash. Dark, ankle length trousers fit into boots two sizes too big. The drape of her clothes, and the ornamentation embroidered on her sash, told Rayna the girl's origins were from across the sea in Ischon. There they cut designs to showcase elegance but not at the sacrifice of movement.

From what Rayna knew about Ischon, all who lived on the isle were trained in the arts of warfare from a young age. The girl in front of her didn't seem to carry the killer instinct Rayna would've expected. For one thing, the way she tracked Rayna was sloppy. Any skilled assassin wouldn't have been so obvious.

This girl kept looking upon her with dark eyes full of wonder. Her features were soft showing the signs of youth and not much battle wear. Rayna leaned back in her chair and kicked her feet up on the table. She didn't want to let on that she knew the girl was eyeing her. While Ryu snuggled in her lap eating slivers of dried meat from her fingers, Rayna watched her watcher.

5

Heavy Sits the Crown

F ine wine and luscious women kept him
entertained. He lauded power over those who
used to laugh at him. The crown rested upon
his head, taken from his father by his own hand. On the
surface, life was good. Why then did Falkon Fourspire
feel more unsettled than before he became king?

The answer to that question came as the servant girl
interrupted Falkon's afternoon indulgence. He bedded
beautiful maidens and drank until his mind grew numb.
Intoxicated and satisfied, Falkon finally relaxed enough
to let worry slip away. Then the girl came calling with a
message from his wife.

Her small knock at the chamber door forced him to
break away from his concubines to answer. The servant
girl's eyes grew wide in shock and then she cast her gaze
to the floor.

"Apologies, my king."

At first, Falkon couldn't understand her discomfort. It took a moment for him to realize he answered the door naked. Staggering into a robe he insisted the girl speak. The quicker he heard the message, the sooner he could ignore it and return to his distractions.

"The queen requests your presence in the throne room," the girl told him.

Falkon gritted his teeth so hard he thought he felt one break off in his mouth. He knew if he ignored the request that Nadiuska would come looking for him. She was a beautiful woman and an impressive ruler. But lately, her demands had become insufferable.

"Very well," Falkon told the girl. Then he turned to the others. "Get out, all of you!"

The women did as he commanded and rushed out of the room. He slammed the door behind them pleased that someone still headed his order. His wife was no longer under his control. But he couldn't let the people of Sandhal know that. He'd only sat the throne for a short time. If word spread across Atharia that the new king showed weakness it would draw usurpers.

Falkon sat on the edge of the bed guzzling the last of the wine from its decanter. His hands were unsteady causing him to spill a portion of it onto his thick beard and across his chest. He was sticky from sweat and wine when he finally lumbered his way into the throne room to greet his wife.

Nadiuska sat upon the dais looking down at him in disgust. Falkon was disgusted at the sight of the monstrosity that was her custom throne. A commission piece that cost him a great amount of gold to have made. It represented one more of Nadiuska's whims that Falkon just couldn't seem to refuse.

No matter how much he tried to argue something always swayed him to her cause. His mind didn't feel like his own anymore. Falkon grew concerned that he may be going mad just like his father had.

"You look positively retched, dear husband," Nadiuska told him.

Her tongue had grown bold in only a short time. If another spoke to Falkon in such a manner he would have it ripped from their head. Somehow he couldn't bring himself to even admonish his queen. But she had no problems lashing out at him. He started up the stairs of the dais to take his place at her side when she stopped him.

"Stay down there while we speak. I don't wish to smell you."

Falkon paused a moment to take in his own scent. She was right, he could do with a perfumed bath. But having his queen point out his faults felt like the disappointing tone of his father cast down on him all over again.

Swaying on drunken legs, Falkon straightened up as

best he could. With shoulders back and head up he tried to control the conversation like a true king would. Nadiuska wouldn't allow him the satisfaction.

As he started to speak she cut him off with a wave of her hand. Suddenly his throat felt dry and his tongue thick. He wanted nothing more than to quench the feeling of sand in his mouth with another drink.

"Do you know why I called on you?" Nadiuska asked.

Falkon did his best to answer. "You want something else that will cost me a small fortune?"

A joke that was mostly true. To date, his new bride made several demands that cut into the kingdom's riches. She even had the builders design her a private room off the gardens for what she called "spiritual reflection." Only Nadiuska and her Daughters of Chaos were allowed inside.

The Saltwood Soldiers had come to Falkon with concerning stories of the sounds emanating from the room at night. When Falkon questioned his wife about it, she dismissed him like so many times before.

At the moment, she was not pleased with his attempts at humor. Dark eyes against a pale complexion gave her an even harder stare. Falkon tried not to buckle under the weight of it but he felt a discomfort growing in his body the longer he looked at her.

"You made me a promise that remains unfulfilled," she told him. When he didn't respond she pushed further.

"Did you not make a solemn vow to me on our wedding day?"

Falkon's head swam with intoxication and dark thoughts. Memories of the past day eluded him let alone the span of time between meeting and marrying Nadiuska. Unsure of what promise she spoke of Falkon thought it best to make up a lie.

"Of course I remember," he said. "I've just been busy with other duties. But I assure you, I shall keep my promise."

"Your duties have consisted of whoring and drinking yourself into an early grave." She continued with a smile which surprised him. "That doesn't concern me in the slightest. However, I came to this retched kingdom for a singular purpose."

She stood looking god-like as she cascaded down the stairs towards him. Her dark robes were offset by subtle hues of lavender and gemstones of amethyst. The length of them trailed behind her emphasizing her regal nature. Inches away from Falkon he felt her words caress his lips.

"The girl," she spoke. "You promised you would bring her to me."

It all came flooding back to him in that moment as though a veil had been lifted from his mind. The dragonslayer. Blonde, built, and a bitch of a thorn in his side. She remained on the loose somewhere in Atharia elusive to capture.

Falkon had all but given up on finding her. His was a life of indulgence now. But Nadiuska grew more impatient each day the girl was not found. Why she sought the slayer she never let on. Only that her capture was imperative. Falkon too owed the girl a debt. But after so much time searching he was ready to give up and move on. Nadiuska would not allow it.

"Yes, the girl, Rayna," he said. "I believe we had a pact to join forces and find her together. You've not held up your end either, my queen."

Nadiuska crooked her eyebrow. "Your boldness surprises me but you are correct. My Howlers are gone, cut down by that fucking barbarian!"

Her voice boomed off the walls like a thunderclap. It rattled the paintings and threatened to knock the bones of a once mighty dragon from its display. She bowed her head to compose herself. Then, unexpectedly, she wrapped her arms around Falkon's neck.

"She's become too strong," Nadiuska whispered. "We need to come together and root her from hiding."

The scent of her was more intoxicating than even the finest wine. His hands moved over her curves and settled on her backside then pulled her body against his own.

"It's been a long time since we've come together."

He leaned in to kiss her and she pressed a finger against his lips. In the short time they'd known each other, Falkon learned his wife desired bloodshed more than sex. Sacrifices aroused her but left him wary. Still, she held an ethereal beauty unmatched by any he'd ever seen...except perhaps Rayna.

"Fetch me the girl first," Nadiuska told him. "Then you'll be rewarded."

Reluctantly, he let his hands slip from her body and stepped back. With no further words Falkon nodded his head and left to do her bidding. Somewhere in a short span of time he'd lost control of his rule to Nadiuska. He didn't have any idea how to get it back. Every time he tried she stonewalled Falkon giving him no recourse.

As he cleaned up and dressed he decided to table the matter for another day. The more pressing issue at the forefront was finding Rayna. Dripping wet from a bath he stared at his reflexion in a full length mirror. His eyes were dull; the skin around them appeared gaunt. He must've aged ten years since he took the throne only a few months prior.

Ruling wasn't as easy as he thought it would be. Falkon longed for the advice of his trusted friend and confidante Valerios. But he'd gone to the grave by Falkon's own sword. Betrayal demanded such an ending to Valerios' story. He sided with the once mighty dragonslayer Rayna. Falkon had no choice but to cut him down.

Remembering the pain of losing his right-hand man cleared the haze from Falkon's mind. He needed to find the girl and bring her to justice. Not only did his queen demand it but the people under his rule did as well. Falkon labeled Rayna an enemy to the throne. Bounties were placed on her head. He could not just continue to let her roam free. Rayna needed to answer for her crimes.

6
Keeper of the Dragon

Rayna was deep into a meal of crisp bacon and honey soaked breads when the watcher finally made her move. She took two bold steps up to the table, squared her hips, and dropped her voice low to sound more menacing.

"Are you the dragonslayer?"

Rayna didn't bother looking up. This was not the time nor place for a fight. She didn't want the attention. Besides, a young girl doing her best to impersonate a warrior wasn't worth spoiling her meal over.

It was a relief to get food at all without the tavern owner giving her trouble. The rest of the patrons were too intoxicated to care whether the famed and feared dragonslayer sat in their midst. But the girl cared a great deal.

She slammed her palm across the table causing Rayna's

mead to spill over the rim of her mug. Then the girl pushed back her cloak to reveal a small dagger at her belt. She inched closer to Rayna and demanded answers to her questions.

"I've come to challenge the mighty dragonslayer. Are you her?"

Rayna took a sip off her mead then set it back down. The second the mug touched the table she reacted with swift and blinding violence. Rayna caught the girl by her exposed wrist and wrenched her arm behind her back. She dragged the girl backwards into the shadow of the room where the others could not see. Then she relieved the small dagger from its sheath and pressed the tip of it under the girl's chin.

"Who sent you?" Rayna asked, her voice low but still demanding.

Compromised with her own weapon used against her, the girl's bravado fell away. She tensed in Rayna's grip but her hands trembled. Apparently she didn't shake from fear rather excitement.

"You are her."

The aggressive tone in her voice had been replaced with a child-like glee. Rayna pressed the dagger harder into the soft flesh to indicate she was not to be fucked with.

"Who sent you?" she asked again.

"No one sent me. I sought you myself."

"Why?"

"So I could challenge the mighty slayer."

"To what end?"

Now the girl's voice fell soft. She grew sullen as she began to reveal pieces of her own sad story.

"I wanted to prove my father wrong and show him my worth."

Rayna felt for the girl. She knew what it was like to want to prove your merit, especially in a world where young women were told to act in a certain manner. Rayna's father died when she was still very young. Her mentor became a man by the name of Darius the Dreaded, leader of a legendary mercenary group the Forsaken Force.

Darius took Rayna in when she had nowhere else to go and raised her as his own. In a group of young men, Rayna fought everyday to stand out from the pack and earn his respect.

Ruminating on the girl's story caused Rayna's grip to lax. It gave the girl enough room to wriggle free. Instead of taking the opportunity to run she instead engaged in the fight once more. Though she felt no threat, Rayna still grew impressed by her opponent's vigor.

She let the girl take a couple of swipes at her as she tried to regain her dagger. Rayna easily sidestepped the advances each time. Then she knocked the girl in the forehead with the handle of the weapon.

"Ouch!"

The girl staggered backwards rubbing her head. Rayna waited to see what her next move would be. If she advanced again, Rayna would have to knock her unconscious. The altercation, as slight as it was, had begun to draw prying eyes. Even if the patrons of Valeuki weren't up to the task of capturing Rayna themselves, there would no doubt be those who would exchange information for gold.

The young girl grimaced, more out of frustration than anger, and started to engage again. Rayna readied herself to catch the girl in a choke hold and put her to sleep. At that moment, Ryu poked his head up. All the while the two women scuffled, he'd been content on eating his scraps of meat. Now that he cleared the plate the dragon wanted to see what all the noise was about.

The moment the girl spotted Ryu she halted in her step and squealed in delight. Rayna had to shoosh her so the others wouldn't look over and see her dragon. The young lady suddenly grew enamored by both Ryu and Rayna.

"It really is you," she began. "The keeper of the dragon."

She began to bow and Rayna waved her off. "No, don't do that."

"I am K'lani," the girl began. "I've come from a great distance to find you."

"My name holds weight across the sea?" Rayna grew surprised.

K'lani beamed with delight. Her cheeks pinking up as she smiled bright like a crescent moon.

"Yes, in my home land you are regarded as a great and brave warrior."

"Where is your home?"

"I'm from Ischon across the sea. A daughter of Emperor Kivu Kazu."

The girl's admission made Rayna flinch for more than one reason. Not only did K'lani's presence bring up memories of an old, dead friend but her reveal brought with it new problems. Now Rayna had more than one treasure with her that any mercenary would be salivating over. Should one of them capture K'lani the Emperor of Ischon would pay a hefty fee for her return.

She didn't know why K'lani traveled such a far distance to find her and Rayna didn't really care. Whether it be guts or glory mattered not. All Rayna cared about was slipping from the tavern with Ryu before the eyes pointed in their direction became blades.

7
Shadowed Legacy

King Falkon needed a win. Not only would finding Rayna appease his queen but the people of Sandhal and all over Atharia would come to respect him. Rayna's name still held weight across the land and even to distant shores. Once they saw how he captured the mighty dragonslayer the people would bow their heads.

He sat in a warm bath for hours trying to come up with a plan. Even as the wine fog lifted from his mind Falkon still couldn't establish an idea. Servant girls fawned over him tending to his every need. They brushed his hair, cleaned his nails, and shaved him as he sat in deep thought.

Not even their young hands on his body distracted him. He was determined to be the leader his father never thought he could be. But in this moment he wished he still had the counsel of Valerios. His wise words always set Falkon on the right course. All Falkon could come up with on his own was to throw more gold at the problem.

Tiring of their touch he waved off the servant girls. Falkon waited until the heavy wooden door closed behind them before calling out for his beloved Xara. It took him several tries until finally a curl of dark smoke appeared at the edge of the bath. It grew in shape and size manifesting into his one true love.

"You came," Falkon lurched forwards and took her hand. "It's been so long since I've seen you. Where have you been?"

She caressed his hand and his cheek. It felt good to feel her touch again. Then she slapped him. It wasn't the playful slaps they often engaged in during their love making. Her strike was hard and intended to hurt him.

Falkon pushed her back causing Xara to fall from the edge of the bath. He emerged soaking wet and enraged intent on stalking her down and having his way with her. But Xara wasn't like the servant girls. She held special gifts that permitted her to travel on air or cloak herself entirely.

Once he reached out to grab her wrist she vanished. Xara also held Falkon's heart like no other before. When she reappeared at the other end of the room he let his anger subside.

"Why did you strike me?" he asked.

"You forget yourself, King Falkon," Xara replied. "My mother is your queen."

Falkon dried himself then draped a silk woven robe over his shoulders. He knew talk of Nadiuska would come up but he would not let it sway him of his desires. Without Valerios in his life, Xara was his only confidante left.

"I do not insult your mother," he explained. "She has been open to our coupling in the past and willingly given her blessing."

Xara's eyes narrowed into slits. "Things are different now."

Falkon knew the reasons as to why without needing to ask the question. Xara and her sister Xiomara were the Daughters of Chaos. They cherished their mother to the point where her wants and needs became theirs as well. Because Falkon had yet to capture Rayna it was impacting his social life as well as his rule over the people.

"I know your mother seeks the slayer though I'm still not sure why," Falkon said. "If anyone should be bothered by the woman Rayna still walking freely on Atharia it should be me."

Xara moved closer to him. "Don't you see? That's exactly what wounds mother. She sees how the loss of your companion weighs heavy on your mind. It pains her that you drown your sorrows in libations rather than ruling with gusto."

As Xara's words invigorated him so too did the caress of her touch on his knotted shoulders. A second set of hands joined in the massage as her sister Xiamara made a sudden appearance.

"We want what mother wants," Xiamara whispered. "To see a strong king set in purpose."

"Yes," Falkon murmured as they relaxed his weary muscles.

"A leader that the people no longer laugh at," Xara added.

Her words brought discomfort even under the soothing touch of their hands. Falkon pushed them away, tightened the belt on his robe, and left the bath. He sensed the girls following him as he made his way to his private chambers.

On any other day he would welcome their nubile, young bodies into his bed. On this day his woe outweighed his desires. Did the people truly laugh at him? Was he still looked upon as a fool the way his father saw him? This could not be allowed.

Falkon went to the large oriel window and looked down upon the masses. From his vantage point he could see all the way into Sandhal Square where most of the daily business took place. The shops bustled with activity and the people meandered about with their day-to-day needs. As dreary as it looked they all owed their existence to King Falkon. It was time he reminded them of that.

Turning from the window he found the Daughters of Chaos still in his presence. They wore masks of mischief as their countenances though Falkon couldn't discern why. He disregarded them and began to dress.

"You may leave me now," he told them.

"As you wish, my king," they replied in unison.

Sometimes the way the girls moved and spoke as mirrors of each other made Falkon's skin prickle in fear. He wasn't fool enough to believe they were average maidens. Something strange and perhaps sinister lurked beneath their bodies. But those bodies were beautiful and his to enjoy. The same went for their mother, Nadiuska, his queen. Though sometimes she needed to be reminded of such things.

For now, Falkon's attention was elsewhere. On their way out he stopped the daughters and levied on them a task. If Falkon were going to solidify his rule he needed to understand why they had failed to find Rayna up to this point. Only one man held the answer to that question.

"Fetch me Coraise Kennethgorian."

8
Across the Sea

Trying to pack up and leave with stealth and haste proved difficult while K'lani fawned all over her. It grew worse as Ryu began to enjoy the attention. He kept crawling out of his satchel and onto the table to stare at K'lani while she talked.

"We need to go," Rayna told him.

She tried to scoop him back into her bag and he snapped at her. It wasn't as aggressive an attack as before but he still managed to nip her thumb. Undaunted, Rayna continued to reach for him but Ryu proved too swift. He darted back and forth across the table until finally running into K'lani's arms.

At first, Rayna thought the girl had snatched her dragon like so many others tried to before. She was prepared to engage in another fight until she realized Ryu ran to K'lani on his own accord. He nuzzled his nose against her palm as she stroked the top of his head.

"He likes me," K'lani exclaimed.

Rayna grimaced. "Traitor."

Her words were meant for Ryu but K'lani took offense. She set the dragon back down and then began a nervous speech she seemed to have set to memory. In just a short span of time she'd gone from a warrior invoking a challenge to a girl begging for guidance.

"Let me go with you. I want to learn everything you know."

"Why would I allow that?"

"Because I'm not cut out for a simple village life." K'lani's gaze drifted upwards as though she were able to look into the future and capture its essence. "I was born to do so much more."

"Go back to Ischon, to your family," Rayna told her as she finally persuaded Ryu back into his satchel. "You'll find purpose in your father's kingdom."

"I don't fit in back home," K'lani replied, her eyes drifting back down into reality. "I want to be a warrior like you."

"I travel alone."

"What about him?"

She pointed at Ryu and he squeaked in regards. Rayna tried to quiet him with some slivers of deer jerky. She didn't want to encourage the girl but Ryu continued to make it difficult. It was almost as if he could understand the conversation and wanted K'lani to come along.

"He's none of your concern," Rayna told her. "We have to go now."

With her belongings packed, her sword at her hip, and Ryu safely at her back they headed out. They had much ground to cover and only a few hours of daylight left. But Rayna's pest continued to follow her outside.

"Where are you headed?"

"Mako. I have a long journey ahead."

"That's in the Shadowed Highlands isn't it? They say no one ever returns from there."

"I did."

K'lani seemed surprised. "You did?"

Rayna grimaced as the girl's excitement grew. What's worse were the incessant questions. Rayna knew what she was doing, trying to pry information from her, but she would never give enough details for the girl to successfully follow her.

"Why by the Source Gods would you want to return to that place?"

"I seek magic."

"Are you going to take the same route you used the last time?"

K'lani started running her hands over Rayna's horse and the saddle pack. She was checking for the type of supplies Rayna carried. Everyone knew that the Shadowed Highlands held very little sunlight. As such, the area grew very cold and traversing it meant specific clothing and weapons were needed.

"I like to study maps and place locations," K'lani continued. "Did you know the current maps spelled my island wrong? It's Ischon with an 'S' but they left it off. So, which route do you usually take to Mako?"

"Don't even think about it."

"About what?"

"Following me," Rayna said. "You think I can't tell when someone is pumping me for information? Makes me wonder if you sad story is true or if you're really just after the bounty. Either way, you don't want to make me mad do you?"

"Of course not. I was just hoping I could learn from you and maybe even teach you some things as well."

Rayna couldn't help but scoff. "I've been traveling these lands alone since I was a twelve-year old girl. What lessons do you think you could impart to me that I don't already know?"

"Well, for instance you shouldn't be feeding Ryu so much salted meat. It will give him the runs."

At her words, Rayna stopped feeding the dragon even though he insisted on finishing the last cured stick of meat. With gentle care she slipped the satchel from off her back and let him loose.

The moment he settled on the ground he broke wind. It was the most noxious smell Rayna ever confronted. Even the horse cried out from the stench. Ryu didn't seem to mind at all. In fact, he tried to reach out for more salted meat.

"Why does he keep wanting to eat if it upsets his stomach?"

"Like many of us we seek the things that are bad for us because they bring us pleasure."

"You're a philosopher as well?"

"I have many skills."

Rayna assessed K'lani head-to-toe. She wore armor that didn't fit. Her skill with weapons was clumsy. She talked far too much to move with stealth. But something about her cried out to Rayna for help. It was almost as if her good friend Valerios brought the two of them together.

"Alright, you can come with us so long as you don't keep asking me questions."

K'lani's face lit up with joy and she moved to hug Rayna. Stepping back from the embrace, Rayna almost fell over Ryu. She scooped him up in one arm and waved K'lani back.

"Don't do that either."

"As you wish, dragonslayer," K'lani said with a small bow of her head. "Silent and no sudden motions. Got it."

"Rayna."

"What?"

"You can call me Rayna."

"Yes, Rayna." K'lani smiled. "And what's your

dragon's name?"

"This is Ryu."

Ryu squeaked out a response as his name was mentioned. That could no longer be considered coincidence. Rayna knew he was starting to understand conversations. How long before a stumble in conversation let him learn she had killed his mother?

"I thought the dragons had all disappeared from Atharia. How did you come to find him?"

The way K'lani specifically mentioned Atharia and not the entire land gave Rayna pause. She wondered if the girl knew more than she was letting on. For now, she was beginning to annoy Rayna with all the questions.

"That's not your concern." Rayna turned to Ryu. "This is a mistake already."

"No, I'll be quiet I promise."

They gathered their things and Rayna repacked the horse. She slipped Ryu onto her back once more and saddled up ready to clear some distance on her journey. Then, another question came.

"Rayna?"

"What is it now?"

"I'm sorry, I just...uh...Do you have another horse?"

Rayna shifted in her saddle to look down on the girl. She looked like a child who had been scolded for stealing bread. Regret flooded over Rayna as she could feel the weight of caring for yet another being on her journey.

For someone who carved a name for herself traveling the lands alone and slaying mighty dragons she sure had gotten soft.

"Come on then," she said, reaching down for K'lani's hand.

Joy washed over the girl's face as she scrambled up on the back of the horse. She didn't even seem to mind staring directly into the dangerous maw of the red dragon. In fact, K'lani took it as an opportunity to bond with Ryu. Once that happened, Rayna knew she would never get rid of her.

"What is the horse's name?" she asked.

"It doesn't have a one."

"No name? That isn't too lucky. You should always name your horse. What about Noblefeet?"

Exasperated with the questions, Rayna indulged her. "Were not calling him that."

"Sir Steadfast?"

"Gusto," Rayna said sharply. "Call him Gusto."

The horse let loose a whinny which prompted K'lani to cheer.

"I think he likes it."

Rayna spurred forth the newly christened Gusto while the rest of the traveling circus sat at her back. Trying to stay out of sight and away from the king's trackers would prove difficult with the group of them ambling about.

9

Dirty Dogs & Dragons

The peasants were revolting. It seemed the people in Sandhal didn't care for their new leader. Coraise laughed as large crowds began to swarm outside in the square. The Saltwood Stronghold, as it was so aptly named, sat high over the city looking down on the little people. But one by one those people began to come together. Soon, they weren't so little any longer.

They made one giant mass, enough to challenge the Saltwood Soldiers if they wanted to. As they started flinging spoiled crops and pig shit towards the castle, Coraise knew a siege was coming soon. Best if he were gone before that happened.

"Why am I here, Falkon?"

"That's King Falkon to you."

Coraise turned round with a smile. "Shall I drop to a knee and kiss your bejeweled fingers or would you prefer I suck your cock?"

King Falkon Fourspire looked like a child playing pretend as he sat in his father's chair wearing his father's robes and attempting to be a ruler. The only thing Falkon had that his father never did were the two beauties on his arms.

They had come to find Coraise and fetch him for their king. At the time he'd thought he'd been imagining things when they appeared. Too drunk to discern otherwise, he let the Sirens sing their song and soon he'd fallen under their spell. Now he was back in front of Falkon awaiting royal commands that he intended to wipe his ass with.

Coraise would've left the castle the moment he sobered up but the beauties kept his interest. They pawed at Falkon like good little lap dogs and all the while a third, most magnificent woman studied Coraise himself.

The queen sat in silence letting her king conduct business. Coraise had been around the world and back again. In that time of travel he'd come to know what true power looked like. It wasn't King Falkon who ruled the kingdom, 'twas his lady.

"Correct me if I'm wrong, Coraise, but haven't you been telling everyone who will listen that you will best the mighty dragonslayer and bring me her head?"

"You are wrong. I believe my exact words were that I'd best the mighty dragonslayer in bed."

He tossed a pity wink towards the quiet queen to which she took offense. So much did it offend her that she excused herself from the room and took the Daughters of Chaos with her. Their departure allowed Falkon to finally locate his balls.

"Did you just wink at my wife?"

"All for show, King Falkon."

Coraise gave him a mock bow then began searching the room for wine. If he were going to be trapped in the castle the least they could do was provide him with libations.

"You might get more of my queen than you can handle, Coraise Kennethgorian," Falkon told him.

"Are you offering?"

Falkon chuckled. "You can't even catch one young girl wandering alone in a forest. A full grown woman the likes of Nadiuska is out of your league."

Coraise prided himself on remaining calm under pressure. He never let idle insults get under his skin. Most battles were won with wits, after all. But Falkon's foolish words got to him.

Maybe it was because he already nursed an aching head from too much wine. Or perhaps it irked him because of the lips which spoke them. Falkon Fourpsire was nothing more than a water dog before his father took the throne. Even then, Falkon as captain of the guards held no real merit. His lackey, and most likely his lover, Valerios the Valiant always stepped in to clean up Falkon's messes.

Valerios was gone. His father was gone. And still Falkon ran his mouth like a man who felt untouchable. Coraise wanted to reach out and squeeze the king's throat until his crown popped from his head. It would be thrilling but he would never make it out of the castle alive after that. And he still owed Rayna twice over for her disrespect of him.

"You caught up with the girl more than once and she bested you both times."

Falkon talked down to him from his throne as though Coraise were nothing better than one of the peasants outside at the gate. He was the leader of the Righteous Wardens, the most dangerous mercenary group since the Forsaken Force walked Atharia. No one talked down to Coraise Kennethgorian and lived.

"Unforeseen circumstances presented themselves," he replied.

Falkon felt the need to correct him. "Excuses."

Coraise bit back his anger so hard he wound up lacerating his own tongue. Still, Falkon continued to chastise his work while simultaneously levying praise on the girl they both sought. Coraise wanted to bring Rayna to her knees for different reasons than Falkon did.

"One lone girl with a magic sword and a battle-scarred eye fought back the entire Righteous Wardens," Falkon continued. "She fell every single one of your mercenaries except for you. Why is that?"

Now the true meaning behind their meeting presented itself. Coraise couldn't help but chuckle as the anger dissipated from his body. He found his goblet of wine upon a large banquet table laid out with a veritable feast.

Before he answered Falkon's question Coraise took his time sampling the fine delicacies and sipping his wine. Only when he was ready did he give a reply.

"You believe I have some sort of arrangement with this woman?"

Falkon dared to join Coraise at the banquet table though he kept a far enough distance. They both sipped from their goblets eyeing each other over the rim waiting for an attack. Only words were used as daggers this day.

"I wouldn't put it past you to profit from both sides," Falkon finally said. "It's the mercenary way. Besides, you've been carrying on about fucking her since you first saw her."

"What can I say, she's a mighty fine specimen," Coraise answered kicking up his boots upon the table. "But you're wrong about the odds. It has never just been Rayna my Wardens and I encountered. Both times she had reinforcements and that is something you should have mentioned yourself, King Falkon."

Falkon leaned back in his chair and set down his wine. "She had help? From whom?"

"Dirty dogs and dragons."

"Enough riddles. Tell me straight."

"I am. The first time we found her Rayna was alone on a trail but not for long. Once we engaged a stocky son-of-a-bitch came to her aide. He clipped at least three of my men with a bow from the bushes and then they stood side-by-side cleaving heads from shoulders. I only came to learn later that her savior was a Night Howler."

"A what?"

"Cursed beings not of this world," Coraise explained. "They are part human and part wolf."

"Sounds familiar," Falkon sounded both frightened and confused as he tried to recall the details of such a beast.

"Now you see what I've been dealing with," Coraise told him. "This is not just some average bounty. These heads you seek have strange powers. Much like your queen and her daughters."

Falkon looked back over his shoulder, then spoke low as though he feared their return.

"Yes, well that is another matter." He turned back to Coraise with more questions. "You said both times Rayna had help. This man-beast remains with her?"

Coraise shook his head. "The dragon saved her the second time."

"The dragon?"

"I watched it burn the faces from my men with its fiery

breath."

"With yourself out of harms way of course."

"A good leader sends scouts first else we wouldn't be having this conversation."

"Still, a dragon and a slayer working in tandem?"

"Dragons are stupid creatures. They do as they're told."

Coraise poured himself more wine and waited. Falkon's silence unnerved him. Once again the king spoke in a hushed tone as though the walls could hear them.

"I believe there is more to it than that," he began. "You have seen her eye?"

Coraise nodded, set his cup aside, and then listened more intently.

"I've seen what she can do when she casts that dragoneye upon her blade," Falkon continued. "No telling what other witchcraft she wields. Perhaps enough to get a dragon to do her bidding."

"And here's the part where you beseech me to seek her head one final time."

"Yes."

"Well then, you should've kept your stories to yourself, good king," Coraise told him. "Because now the price just doubled."

He straddled the line of good judgment but it kept things interesting. Many said that Falkon was quick to

anger and would order a beheading should someone
look sideways at him. Coraise wasn't concerned with the
king's temper. He knew he had Falkon by the balls. For
whom else could capture a warrior woman the likes of
Rayna the Dragonslayer?

Still, Falkon would not give Coraise what he asked for
without putting up a fight. He wouldn't expect anything
less from the so-called ruler of Sandhal. But Coraise
wasn't going back out after Rayna without getting more
riches as his reward. When he explained why it seemed
to soothe King Falkon's nerves.

"I need to replace my men. That's going to take bribery.
The rest of it, well that's you bribing me to go out after
this woman again after you so much as told me she's a
witch."

"I'd be a fool to reward failure," Falkon argued.

"I haven't failed," Coraise told him. "I've just been
regrouping."

"In a brothel?"

"If you believe there is someone else that can handle
the challenge then by all means bore them with this
conversation."

Coraise rose from his chair and finished his wine. He
smiled at Falkon and started towards the exit. His moves
were meticulous and done in an effort to create a sense
of urgency. Either Falkon would pay up or he'd lose his
best chance at getting the girl. Coraise had no real

intention of leaving but he needed Falkon to think he was.

He continued his slow, measured tread towards the door waiting for Falkon to call him back. Instead, Queen Nadiuska is the one who halted Coraise. She stepped in his path from seemingly nowhere and looked him over.

"Pay the man, Falkon," she said, her jewel-like eyes still fixated on Coraise. "He's going to earn every bit of it."

Usually the hard stare and her choice of words would be an open invitation for a seduction. But Nadiuska's stare felt different. It was as if she were assessing him in a manner that ran much deeper than physical. Then she stroked his cheek and the tingle that remained on his skin made Coraise take a step back.

There was madness in her eyes. A deep seeded hatred for the world of men. Whatever story she spun to sit the throne sprang from lies. But Coraise wouldn't dare call her on it; not when he could sense what she was capable of. Fortunately, King Falkon finally agreed to terms.

"Very well, you'll get your gold," he said, stepping between them and taking his wife's hand in his own. "But I expect success this time around."

No more words were spoken from the queen. She need not say anything for Coraise to know that another failure would mean his head. He smiled, bowed, and set off to gather ten good men who would be capable of capturing the hunter of hunters.

10
Defiance

Nadiuska watched the mercenary as he left. His large, lean frame and eyes of a cold-hearted killer intrigued her. Given proper motivation Coraise Kennethgorian could be an unstoppable juggernaut of chaos. She would keep a close watch on that one.

Falkon, on the other hand, already started gloating. Coraise hadn't even gathered his men together yet and already Falkon proclaimed victory. He kissed Nadiuska on the cheek and embraced her in a tight squeeze. His scent was an odious mix of wine and perspiration. But Nadiuska smiled and played along to humor him.

"You see that, dear wife? I've taken care of matters with Rayna."

"Very good, my king," she told him. "And her pet?"

The mention of the dragon gave Falkon pause. This

angered Nadiuska. He could dance around the
complexity of killing the dragonslayer all he wanted but
when it came to the dragon itself, Nadiuska held no
patience.

"I. Want. That. Dragon."

She spoke slow and deliberate so the words would
penetrate his thick skull like a mallet to the head. Falkon
scratched the stubble of a beard growing upon his face.
One more thing Nadiuska found unappealing about him.
Then he waved off her grievance as though it were
already taken care of.

"I'm certain Coraise will come through this time."

"Make sure he does," she warned. "If I don't get my
dragon I will not be pleased."

All the bravado left Falkon's face. "It will be done even
if I have to ride out myself."

Nadiuska stifled a laugh. To think that a man whose
best days were behind him, if he ever had any at all,
could find victory over a well seasoned warrior was
amusing. But she didn't want to break his spirit just yet.
So, she obliged Falkon in his fantasy and played the role
of queen once more.

"You needn't do that, husband. Just ensure the
renewed Righteous Wardens do not return empty
handed."

"I'll have Coraise reminded of your request and of
what will happen in failure."

"Very good." She took his hand in hers. "Now shall we let the public know that the slayer shall be brought to justice soon?"

Falkon nodded. "Indeed."

They walked out onto the balcony as a unified team in front of the angry peasants. Nadiuska looked over their faces pressing against the gates of the castle and demanding justice.

They didn't care so much for their former king; there's was a mourning for the beloved Valerios the Valiant. The former right hand and counsel to Falkon. Nadiuska wondered what the people would do if they knew the truth. If they found out that their current king had been the one to slay Valerios, and not the dragon girl, they would storm the castle and drag him out.

But an odious web of lies spun by the king himself had them raging for Rayna's blood rather than his own. Nadiuska had to give him credit. It was quite a good plan. Get the people all over the land of Atharia seething over such actions and Rayna would have nowhere to hide.

The girl had done a fine job of eluding them so far but her luck would soon run out. Nadiuska would keep throwing obstacles in her way until she slipped up. But the queen needed to be careful. She couldn't expend too much energy casting so far out. It would drain her of magic and she would need to refill with dragon's blood sooner than she wanted to.

For now, the tingle of it still coursed through her veins. She felt unimaginable power the likes she'd not known in countless ages. Once the red dragon was in her grasp she would never want for power again.

Falkon raised up their arms to seek praise from the people. Instead, they jeered him in his failure. Nadiuska couldn't really blame them. He'd kept none of his promises since taking the throne. But then, the wants of the people meant nothing to her. She simply needed the distraction while she gathered her power and made her plans.

"Why do they not love me?" he asked her.

"Forget about gaining their favor. They should fear you." She stroked his cheek. "My love is all you need. Now show these fools why they should bow to their king."

"How?"

"Make an example of one."

"What do you mean?"

Falkon held the same sheepish nature as those that stood outside the gates. He didn't carry the strength of a lion needed for a leader. No matter; Nadiuska would lead him through. She'd been doing the same to his father for months before his passing. Manipulation was one of her strongest weapons. That's how she managed to puppet Rayna in the first place. Now it was Falkon's turn.

"Pick one from the crowd and bring him forth."

They scanned the group of people together until Rayna found the perfect one of the sheep to make her point. An older man who showed the weariness of battle on his face but a glimmer of hope still resting behind his eyes. She would extinguish that hope along with the rest of them.

"That one." She pointed to the man as he stood with the others silent in his disdain for the royal house. "He's the one."

"Cyrus? But he used to serve with the Saltwood Soldiers."

Nadiuska smiled. "Even better."

But Falkon wasn't seeing the beauty of her plan and he didn't agree with the forceful approach. He lowered her hand and took it in his once more.

"Let me reason with them. Once they hear that I have things in order they'll calm down." He gave her a knowing smile and then tried to pander to the public. "People, I bring news that will comfort you in your beds tonight. My men are on their way to collect the dragonslayer and bring her back here. It is my vow as your king that she will pay for the crimes brought against her!"

With Nadiuska's hand still cupped in his, Falkon raised up their arms together awaiting the cheers of the people.

Instead, they only grew louder. Their ire grew stronger. Many began to throw fruit and rocks. They spit in his direction even though they could not reach him on the balcony.

One of them rose up in defiance. "You're a false king!"

"Your father would never have allowed this!" another yelled.

The mockery was getting to Falkon, especially the words about his father. Nadiuska reveled in it because she could see the anger beginning to build in him. If he found his own way to the path she needed him on perhaps her puppet would be useful a little longer.

It was when Cyrus himself spoke up that Falkon truly grew enraged.

"Why do you send mercenaries instead of the royal guard?"

Falkon couldn't answer that question without sounding like a coward. He had kept the Saltwood Soldiers close by to protect him in case the threats grew into violence. Nadiuska knew this, and apparently so did many in the village. She waited to see what Falkon would do given this judgment of his rule. He did not disappoint.

"That one," he called to his soldiers below. "Bring him forth!"

The Saltwood Soldiers did as commanded. Nadiuska made certain of that. Whether by a small dusting of a spell, or using her daughters to persuade them to the cause, the soldiers had become mere shells of the men they were. They would obey like trained dogs.

In order to grab Cyrus and bring him forth they had to open the gates. To do that, they started beating back the crowd until they dispersed enough for the soldiers to get through. Two of them grabbed Cyrus by the arms and dragged him into the square.

He still had some fight left in his old body and he tried to break free. But after slipping loose one arm, and bloodying a guard's nose, he was taken down. They clubbed him into submission and forced him to his knees.

Nadiuska could see Falkon wavering in his resolve. Perhaps some humanity still lay beneath the surface of his lust for women and power. But he would need to make an example of this man if ever the people of Sandhal, and all of Atharia, were to take his rule seriously.

"He dares to question your orders," she whispered, a kick of a spell secreting from her lips to his ears.

"You dare to question my orders?" Falkon repeated.

"No," Cyrus replied. "I question your claim to the throne!"

The crowd erupted in a mixed chorus of cheers and jeers. Some townsfolk tried to scale the gates and were met with spear jabs to their ribs. Others pleaded for Cyrus to be shown mercy. Nadiuska had other ideas in mind for Falkon to carry out.

Leave one bad seed in a bunch and it will begin to infect the entire crop. Cyrus needed to be rooted out before others began to listen to his concerns. And with a former member of the Saltwood Soldiers leading them a mutiny would soon follow. Better to weed out the bad crop now.

"Execute him," she whispered again.

Falkon rubbed his temples. His head ached as his mind tried to fight off her persuasive words. A quick wave of her hand summoned the Daughters of Chaos. The three of them joined their powers together and again whispered the command. This time Falkon did not fight it. He heard the words as his own and repeated them to the guards below.

"Execute him!"

On his order the crowd of peasants erupted. First, a gasp then a culmination of shouting. All of it went unheard. Once the orders were laid out the soldiers did as they were told. Never mind that some may have served with Cyrus before. They could not disobey their king. Nadiuska made certain of that.

Normally, the be-headings took place in the cells. But to make a proper example of Cyrus, his head fell right there in the courtyard where all could see. Nadiuska watched in delight as the executioner was brought forth. While he sharpened his axe, the other guards forced Cyrus in place.

His chest rested on the executioner's block with his neck extended over it. The old man seemed to be saying some sort of prayer though Nadiuska could not make it out. If he sought saving from the Source Gods he would be waiting a long time. They did not dare show themselves while she walked the land. Nadiuska laughed at the thought of it until Cyrus spoke louder.

"Rayna will come for you!" He shouted in defiance of his fate. "She'll make you all pay for your corruption of the throne!"

A chill rushed over Nadiuska like a cold blast of air upon her skin. Had this old soldier somehow communed with the gods and seen a future to come? Her concern mixed with anger at his defiant tone and she lauded the next command herself.

"Kill him!"

The guards obeyed and the old man finally fell silent. As Nadiuska reveled in the bloodshed and the gasps of fear coming from the crowd, Falkon distracted her. He vomited at the sight of Cyrus' head rolling around on the ground. Another sign of weakness from the soft king. Nadiuska used it to further implant herself as the true ruler.

"You've done well, husband. The people of Sandhal now know their fates hinge on your every word."

She motioned for her daughters to take Falkon into their care. They took him by the arms, caressing his cheeks and massaging his neck until he fell obedient.

"Rest now," Nadiuska told him.

Falkon complied without the need for a spell to persuade him. He could not stand the aggressive nature that came with the ruling class. His was a life of decadence and debauchery. This is why Nadiuska sought his father as her puppet initially.

King Favian held a legacy of a pirate turned ruler by any means necessary. His rule was ruthless and manipulative. He'd been the perfect patsy for Nadiuska's plan to draw out the dragonslayer. Unfortunately, the wench somehow swayed Favian to her cause and he began to break free of Nadiuska's spell.

Only then did she set her sights on Falkon. Sending in her daughter Xara first to seduce him. Then, when Nadiuska felt strong enough, she traveled down from the Majestic Mountains to complete the job. All that remained to provide her with the true power she sought was Rayna and her dragon pet.

11
Kappas

Some of the most hardened warriors often spoke of the drudgery life on the road brought with it. They grew melancholy in their loneliness which caused them to make mistakes befriending any who seemed like good company. More often than not those warriors wound up robbed, raped, or murdered.

Rayna preferred the silence. She liked long rides where she could think on past deeds, future plans, and simply meditate on her experiences. How she missed her precious solitude.

K'lani hadn't stopped speaking from the moment they set out from Valeuki. At first, Rayna tried to ignore her but as they got further out into parts unknown the chatter grew distracting. Finally, she informed K'lani she hadn't been listening in hopes it would keep her quiet. The girl responded by telling Rayna the conversation hadn't been meant for her but for Ryu.

At first, Rayna thought the girl made up a lie so as not to be embarrassed. Then she realized K'lani spoke the truth. Ryu was her audience and he didn't seem to mind. From that point on Rayna had no choice but to let the conversation continue, one-sided though it might be.

On the outset, K'lani spoke to Ryu about nothing particularly interesting. Most of it seemed to revolve around food or her misadventures trying to locate Rayna. Only when K'lani began talking of her family did it catch Rayna's ear.

"The Isle of Ischon is made of rules...at least for the women," she began. "And if you were born of a royal house those rules became even stricter. My sister Kemi was older and prettier than me. She got doted on because of her beauty. I always fought for her scraps. Eventually, it wasn't enough for me so I left."

Rayna wanted to stay out of it but ghosts haunted her. She could hear the words of her friend Valerios speaking of his beautiful Kemi who awaited him on Ischon. They were betrothed to marry in a deal made between Emperor Kivu Kazu and the former King Favian. Rayna always found it strange that the king offered up Valerios, a glorified scholar, rather than his own son Falkon.

After getting to know both men on the ill-gotten journey that led into her current predicament, she came to realize the reason why. Valerios was a man of integrity, loyalty, and honor. That's so hard to find in this world. Even King Favian recognized these traits in him that his own son did not possess.

It made Rayna tear up thinking that Valerios would never make it back to his lover. The way K'lani spoke on matters told her that no one on Ischon had been informed of his passing. She took a deep breath and decided to divulge that information herself. Valerios would've wanted Kemi to know.

But as she started to speak something spooked the horse. He reared back so high almost all of them were thrown from the saddle. Rayna had to bear down into his neck and angle him back onto all fours.

Once she regained control of her steed the next move was to scan the area. They were deep into the wilderness with nothing but sprawling acres of woods surrounding them. Any manner of creature could be hiding within the trees ready to jump out.

"What is it?" K'lani whispered.

"I don't see anything but that doesn't mean there isn't something there," Rayna responded.

"I'm ready!"

The girl had drawn two short blades Rayna hadn't noticed before. As extensive a traveler that she was, Rayna never made it out to Ischon. The more time she spent with K'lani told her they had many tricks she needed to learn there. For now, Rayna had her own tricks to evade a surprise attack.

"Put those away and hold on tight."

For once, K'lani did as she was told. When Rayna felt her secure, with Ryu steady as well, she spurred Gusto to charge. The horse obliged her and darted forwards. More than likely he wanted to escape those unfamiliar woods just as much as they did.

Staying tight to the dirt trail, Rayna moved with Gusto in a fluid race through the trees. She could hear K'lani grunting behind her as the speed picked up and the bumps increased. Ryu remained calm as he was used to the erratic nature of their travel.

Finally, the breaking of light shone through the trees and marked the edge of the forest. Rayna spurred Gusto harder anxious to leave behind whatever lurked in the shadows. Inches from freedom she realized too late that the enemy was not behind them but all over them.

As they charged the exit, one of the creatures stepped out in front. He spun a large bamboo staff over his head and then angled it down to strike at Gusto's legs. Rayna tried to rear him back but it was too late.

The strike pitched the horse forwards and sent the lot of them spilling out over the forest floor. Rayna rolled right up to the feet of her attacker. She looked up into his hideous face and was taken aback.

His features were a mix of human and and some form of reptile. Dark green scales replaced his skin while human eyes stared down at her. Then he pulled a mind-scrambler by opening his mouth and speaking with a soft, polite tone of voice.

"Greetings, dear girl."

His reptilian lips pulled back into something of a smile exposing row upon row of of pointed teeth. Then his countenance quickly grew darker. His pupils flashed into slits and a growl escaped him. With all the rage he could muster, the being struck Rayna atop the head with the bamboo staff and knocked her unconscious.

12
Shifting Alliances

C oraise did not waste time rounding up new members for the Righteous Wardens. He knew where the most vile cutthroats in the land frequented. Many of them would be willing to take the job just to spill some blood.

With his team in place they geared up and started on their way. No sense sticking around when there was work to be done. Picking up Rayna's trail would take time. At least, that's the excuse Coraise gave his new crew. In reality, he wanted to get as far away from the Saltwood Stronghold as he could. The look that Queen Nadiuska gave him still burned into his soul.

"The faster we find this bitch and turn her over, the quicker we can spend our earnings!"

The Righteous Wardens saluted the speech with swords held high. Next, they started out towards the last place Rayna had been seen around Valeuki. She was a good tracker herself but she'd grown sloppy. Perhaps the burden of having a bounty on her head tripped her up. But Coraise wasn't underestimating her this time. He'd made that mistake before.

Rayna may be youthful but she had amassed a great deal of experience in her twenty years. She had many skills but Coraise still knew he could best her with a proper plan. Routing their way through the Mammoth Woods that plan came into view.

Scuttling through the brush with a limp in his step was a man of dark hair and solid build. His skin carried char marks across the upper arms and back. A portion of his long beard had burned away as well. Coraise at once recognized him as the fighter who aided Rayna at their first encounter. If not for this man's interference they would've captured the girl already. Coraise thought about snatching the man by the feet and dragging him behind his horse until he perished.

"Ho there," the man called out.

He tried to raise his arm in a show of friendship and winced from his injuries. Seeing a sign of weakness, Coraise scrapped his plans of vengeance. The man could be useful to them in their quest.

"Ho there," Coraise replied. "You look as though you've seen better days, friend."

"Indeed I have."

"If there's trouble ahead we would be grateful to know of it."

"You'll only find trouble out past these woods if you seek it intentionally."

Coraise motioned his team into an easy formation. They slowly encircled the wounded man while Coraise watched how he would react. He kept an air of friendliness though he readied himself for an attack.

"What trouble did you seek?" Coraise asked him.

The man laughed. "That of the female persuasion."

The Righteous Wardens laughed along with him. Coraise chuckled as well though he continued to watch the man waiting to see if he were about to make a move. He did not. Instead, he spun a story to keep them from killing him.

"I admit that I caused her some strife and she retaliated."

"By burning you?"

"Well, that was an unfortunate combination of wrong place and wrong time."

"That does sound unfortunate," Coraise told him. "But perhaps we can help you rectify your situation."

"How could you do that?"

"By finding this woman and bringing her to justice. You're standing in the presence of the Righteous Wardens. It's what we do."

The man flexed his fingers several times as though he sought a phantom weapon. But rather than launch an ill-advised attack, he continued to converse with them.

"They call me 'Defiant' Damaris de Paz," he said. "My friends just call me Paz."

"Well met, Damaris. I am Coraise Kennethgorian the leader of the Righteous Wardens. Now that we're acquainted what's say we get you healed up and head after that woman who wronged you?"

"I don't think that's a good idea. A man carrying the moniker of 'defiant' probably wouldn't fit in well with a group of righteous men."

"Righteous in name only. Besides Paz, we're after the same woman. It's best if we travel together."

"I doubt that," Paz smiled. "You look like a man who enjoys the company of exotic beauties whereas I settle for frumpy bar maidens."

Coraise trotted his horse up closer. He leaned into the saddle to look down on Paz as he spoke softly and with detailed accuracy.

"She wears a dirty brown eye patch. Her body is well-muscled. She carries a large broadsword that can be set into flame with just a look. And she has a dragon."

As Coraise described Rayna he watched Paz's face flinch. Then his eyes flashed from light to dark but only for a moment. A growl came from deep in his throat and he bared teeth that now resembled that of a wolf.

From their vantage point, the Righteous Wardens only saw them carrying on a conversation. Coraise continued to let them believe that while he laid out an ultimatum for Paz.

"I know you traveled with Rayna," he said. "At some point you crossed her and she burned you with her sword or the little dragon did it himself. I don't care why. All I care about is finding her.

Either you use that canine sense of smell you have and help us find her or I have no use for you. If I have no use for you then I'm going to wait until you shift into your other form before I slay you so that my team can make new fur coats out of your hide. How does that sound?"

"You know alot about me."

"That I do."

"Then I'd be a fool to turn you down." Paz paused to sniff the air. "Who sent you? Queen Nadiuska?"

His question made Coraise uneasy. With eye motion alone he told his troops to ready themselves. Continuing to speak with Paz, he remained calm but curious.

"I'm here on royal order. How did you know that?"

"You have her stink all over you as if she watches from afar."

A chill ran up Coraise's spine at Paz's words. Knowing the queen kept watch felt like the sands in an hourglass dissipating at double speed. He could not fail to bring Rayna back this time.

"Interesting gift you have."

"I'd call it a curse."

"Still, we could use you in the Righteous Wardens."

"You mean past this quest?"

"Perhaps. Do we have an agreement?" Coraise asked.

Paz thought about it for a moment then gave his reply. "I do owe Rayna. So, yes. We have an agreement."

Coraise made a point of slipping from his saddle and facing Paz like a man. He towered over most men and used that height advantage to intimidate them. Paz seemed unfazed by it. He extended his badly burned arm and Coraise grasped his hand to signify a united front.

When they locked eyes the human man stared back. But Coraise knew the wolf still lurked just beneath the surface. He would watch 'Defiant' Damaris de Paz closely on this journey.

13
Sweet Meat

T he smell of roasting meat woke Rayna from
her forced slumber. Her head ached and the
pain radiated down her neck into the deep
musculature of her shoulder. It was dark save for some
torchlight that cast shadows upon large rock walls.

From what she could make out at first glance she sat in
a cavern of some sort. K'lani was huddled next to her,
both of them bound by the hands and feet. Paces away
the strange reptilian creatures were roasting something
over an open flame.

Rayna's pulse intensified as she panicked to locate Ryu.
If the creatures were cooking him for supper all hope
was lost. Rayna would've failed her mission. Then, she
would gladly follow Ryu into eternity but not before
taking a few of the reptilian bastards with her. Sensing
her distress, K'lani tried to comfort her.

"It's not Ryu."

The wash of relief almost knocked Rayna back into unconsciousness. She leaned against the stone wall as best she could trying to catch her breath and fight back tears. The gratitude she felt for Ryu's safety was quickly extinguished when she learned what they were cooking on the spit.

"It's Gusto," K'lani explained. "They slaughtered him while you were out."

Anger twisted Rayna's face and she flexed against her bonds trying to break free. The ropes were thick and she didn't yet have her full strength back. Looking out across the expanse of the cavern Rayna saw little that could aide her.

They'd taken her scaled armor, sword, and dagger. The only visible weapons were strapped to the belts of their captors. Long, twisted swords that held a wide curve to them.

"Where are our weapons?" she asked K'lani. "Where is Ryu?"

"They found no use for either and left them at the edge of the forest."

"You mean he's out there alone?"

"I'm afraid so."

"What are those things?"

"Have you ever heard about a polite and proper monster that is also evil and extremely dangerous?"

"I've known human enemies who try and lull you with proper manners only to turn on you when they see fit," Rayna said. "But I've traveled a great deal and never crossed such a hideous hybrid such as these creatures."

"Kappas," K'lani explained. "Reptile-type monsters with certain human features. They present immediate danger to both animals and humans alike."

"Then why did they spare Ryu?"

"I didn't catch all of the conversation but I believe it's because he's a scaled being and they won't eat their own."

The dangers of their predicament finally presented themselves clearly to Rayna. She pressed her back further into the wall as though she could become a permanent part of it. That would be preferred to the alternative.

"These Kappas mean to eat us?"

K'lani nodded then bowed her head until her chin rested against her chest. She seemed forlorn. Given their circumstances it was expected. But her melancholy came from a different source than the anticipation of being the Kappas' next meal.

"I tried to fight them off," she muttered. "When they struck you down I did my best to get us to safety. But there were too many of them."

Rayna nudged her with an elbow. "I believe you but we're not beaten yet so don't give up."

Their conversation caught the attention of what must be the leader of the Kappas. He strolled from the fire and approached them with a plate of meat in his webbed hands. As he stepped closer, Rayna recognized him as the same Kappa that struck her in the head.

"Are you ladies hungry?" he asked. "We have plenty."

"Then you don't need to keep us," Rayna told him. "Just loose our binds and we'll be on our way."

"I'm afraid I cannot do that."

"Why not?"

"You see, nothing is sweeter than the taste of human flesh," the Kappa explained. "Especially the nether regions. Those are always the most succulent."

With that his strange, scaly fingers moved up Rayna's thigh until he cupped her groin. His hand lingered there threatening to slip inside her loincloth to fondle her bare flesh. Rayna refused to give him the satisfaction of emotion he was trying to draw from her. K'lani felt the discomfort for both of them and she drew the Kappa leader's attention away with a question.

"Why feed us if you just mean to kill us?"

"We don't want to be rude," he responded. "We're nothing if not gracious hosts. Besides, the fatter the pig the tastier the dish."

With that his eyes flashed to slits and his lips peeled back to reveal double rows of razor sharp teeth. He snapped his jaws towards them in aggression coming inches from Rayna's face. Then he stopped and looked her over.

"What's that on your eye?" he asked.

She tried to turn her cheek but the reptilian hand reached out and forced her still. Inches from his foul smelling hide, Rayna shivered from the prospect of dark magic that wafted from him.

The stink of the charred horse on a plate in front of her almost made Rayna gag as well. His snout plumed hot air from his nostrils as he examined her features. The creature was looking upon her eyepatch with dismay. Clawed fingers reached out and snatched the covering off her face to reveal the dragoneye beneath.

The Kappa shrank back and snapped his jaws several more times. Then he shouted for the others to join him. They hurried from their dinner and circled around as he pointed towards Rayna.

"This one is tainted," he said. "She has the look of a dragon but the features of a human girl."

"An abomination!" another cried out.

Rayna laughed. "You're one to talk."

"Our race is pure," the leader told her. "You have muddied your blood with another not of your kind. We cannot dine on such impurity. Take her outside and kill her. I will not have tainted blood shed in my home."

The Kappas cut the bonds on Rayna's feet and forced her up. Being restrained in a seated position on the ground for so long left her legs weak. She couldn't find her footing and they were forced to drag her from the caverns. Rayna looked back to see the leader toying with K'lani. He stroked her skin and pet her hair like he was checking out livestock.

"This one will do nicely," he said, split tongue darting from his mouth with hunger and desire.

Two of the Kappa clan escorted Rayna from the bunker they called home. They argued among themselves as though she weren't even in their presence. Dismissing her as unworthy would be their last mistake.

"I wanted to feast on those muscles," the fatter of the two said.

"The meat would be too tough anyway," the skinnier one argued. "Better to save room for the porcelain skinned beauty in there, yesss?"

They both agreed that K'lani appeared to be the more tender morsel. Rayna heard just about enough of their culinary banter. She waited until they brought her into a clearing before reacting. But when they pushed her outside she paused in surprise.

Miles of deep, red sand with a blazing sun above them told her they were in the Red Waste. A dangerous desert spanning its nothingness in all directions. It had claimed many lives of those who inadvertently wandered too deep inside. Somehow these creatures had burrowed their way beneath the sands and structured a home there.

Rayna was forced on her knees to ready her for execution. The fatter Kappa took a look at her face one more time. He examined her eye then ran his scaly fingers over her cheeks and jaw.

"A shame this meat has to go to waste," he turned to look at the other and begged him to reconsider. "What if I just took a taste?"

Always one to capitalize on an opening, Rayna took a taste of her own. She wasn't sure how tough the skin would be considering all the scales covering it but she bit anyway. Aiming at the throat she caught a fat pad that lined the larynx. Chomping and tearing with all the strength she could bring to her jaws, Rayna managed to rip open a wound.

Blood darker than night splashed out across the sand and instantly sizzled under the hot sun. The Kappa stumbled back clutching at his throat and gurgling as he tried to scream. Rayna hopped to her feet to continue the assault but his companion engaged attack first. He moved so fast she didn't have a chance to avoid him completely.

Using the scimitar styled weapon he caught her across the belly into scar tissue of a previous wound at her side. The cut doubled her over. Rather than take the opportunity to finish her off the Kappa checked his friend instead. The larger one already lay dead. Another victim for the Red Waste to swallow up.

Enraged at the death of his companion, the slim Kappa retaliated with haphazard swings driven by vengeance. For intelligent creatures they hadn't learned how to harness their emotions well. Rayna used it to her advantage.

The next time the Kappa struck she angled her body so the ropes securing her arms took the hit. They frayed just enough from the cut to allow her to rip them off. Surprised by her strength the Kappa waited a beat before engaging again.

His speed and agility far surpassed Rayna's own especially as blood continued to pump from her fresh wound. The coarse sand beneath the Kappas' feet didn't hinder his movement and he pounced on her again.

Rayna relied on her reflexes to maintain distance from the arcing blade. She dodged several forward slashes and a single thrust before returning attack. Unarmed she had to fall back on hand-to-hand combat. A barrage of strikes to the Kappas' small, round snout didn't cause the damage Rayna hoped for.

The Kappa retaliated with a backhand across her face. It felt like a wet blanket slapping her skin. The blow stung enough to distract her from the follow up attack. He brought his knee up into her ribs and the cut that lay there. Rayna spit blood from her mouth before collapsing to all fours on the ground.

The Kappa had her beat until she opted for foul play.

When in a fight for survival one does whatever is necessary. She palmed a clump of sand and flung it at the Kappa's face. To her chagrin, the eyes enacted a membrane over the pupils to block the attack.

Rayna defeated dragons, shifter beasts, and Shadax. Yet, one skinny Kappa gave her the fight of her life. He arced the blade of the sword down intent to chop off her head. She fell back just before the strike but not enough to avoid contact completely.

The blade caught her on the upper shoulder where her dragon armor no longer sat to protect her. Rayna cried out which made the Kappa shriek with joy. He felt victory coming and relished in it a bit too much. Rayna crawled on her belly across the sand and felt every tiny grain of it embedding into her wound.

Dancing across the sand after her the Kappa leaped onto her back. He bit down hard onto her already damaged shoulder. The rows of razor-sharp teeth in his mouth locked into her skin until he tore a chunk of it free and spat it out. Then he stood and screamed to the sky.

"You were right, Arnacus! She tastes delicious!"

His fallen comrade Arnacus lay paces from them with his sword at his side. Using what strength she had left in her legs and back, Rayna bucked the skinny Kappa off her. He fell hard but recovered quickly. In two quick steps he was on her again but this time she was armed as well.

A roll across the sand brought her to the body of Arnacus where she relieved him of his weapon. It wasn't Bhrytbyrn but it would do the job. The Kappa grimaced at her and began to flee back towards the sanctuary beneath the sands. Rayna knew that if he reached reinforcements she would not survive. She only hoped that K'lani wasn't spinning on a spit down below.

With her wounds pulling blood and strength from her, Rayna couldn't catch the Kappa in time. Instead, she used the sword and tossed it at him. The blade caught him between the shoulders throwing him chest first on the sand. He wriggled there with the blade still sticking out of his back.

As Rayna staggered over she heard a strange hissing coming from his mouth. Undaunted, she pressed the handle of the blade down deep pinning him into the ground. Finally, he stopped wriggling.

Beaten and bloody, Rayna collected both swords and headed down to get K'lani. She wasn't about to leave the girl at the mercy of these mutants. Besides, she owed the rest of them for eating her horse.

14
Buried Deep

C oraise allowed for Paz to eat and get treatment for his wounds. Then they resumed their search for Rayna and her pet dragon. Paz would be a fool to lead them in the wrong direction. The Righteous Wardens were trackers in their own right. Coraise could sense if the shifter altered the facts.

For the most part, Paz did as asked. At times, Coraise thought he saw hesitation from the man as though he wanted to lie but couldn't. As their travel continued they happened upon signs of an altercation. Now it no longer mattered what Paz wanted to do. They found Rayna, or what was left of her.

Her signature massive broadsword lay in the dirt and leaves as though abandoned by its owner. Coraise knew the woman would never depart with such a magnificent weapon unless forced to.

He left the saddle and took up the blade. The heft of it was considerable even in his hands. It made him admire Rayna more for her skill with it.

"Split up and look around," he told his crew. "She's close, I know it."

"You're wrong," Paz said coming up beside him. "Rayna was here but no longer."

"Why do I feel as though you're trying to protect her in some way?" Coraise asked.

"I'm telling you the truth," Paz argued. "There was a fight here. You can tell by the imprints in the dirt and the crushed vines of the forest floor. She was overpowered and taken."

Coraise examined the area himself and found the same markers that Paz did. He grit his teeth in aggravation. If someone captured Rayna before them it would not only cost Coraise the bounty but possibly his head.

"Wardens, gather up," he called. "Someone else has taken our girl as their own. We cannot allow that. Let us find these bastards and collect our rightful bounty."

His group agreed. "Here, here!"

Even Paz lamented they needed to continue following the trail to find her. Though Coraise wondered whether it were concern rather than vengeance that guided Paz towards Rayna. After tucking the broadsword into the belt at his side Coraise saddled up and led on.

Their journey brought them to the edge of the forest

where the Dragon's Backbone split the world of Atharia in half. The massive stone structure had been constructed as a deterrent by the former King Cullen. He envisioned the enormous wall eventually wrapping all of Atharia to keep invading forces out. But the wall took too much time and cost too much to build. What remained effectively cut the country in half and stunted supply runs until rerouting efforts culminated.

At the moment, it kept Coraise and his men from progressing forwards at a swift pace. It would take considerable time they didn't have to scale the wall and get to the other side.

None of it made any sense. According to Paz, the trail ended there at the base of the wall. He sniffed the air and scanned the grounds but saw little else to go on.

"Did they scale it?" Coraise asked aloud.

"From what I sensed back there in the brush, Rayna was dragged away," Paz explained. "She didn't walk out on her own which means climbing with her in tow would be next to impossible."

Coraise pressed his palm against the worn brick to judged its grip. He looked up the face of the wall until it disappeared high into the clouds above. None could scale the Dragon's Backbone with prey on their back unless they were prepared for it.

"Who do we think took her?" he asked, seeking each of his soldiers for their best answer.

Most of the same thoughts came to mind: bandits from Kartha or pirates. Some even swore the Forsaken Force were involved. Coraise heard rumors that the group of thieves still operated in the shadows. If this were true, their skills would be a formidable match for Rayna. But Paz gave an opinion that differed from the others and surprised Coraise.

"No human took her," he said pointing to the trail marks in the dirt. "Creatures with long tails and webbed feet left tracks all around this spot."

Coraise shrugged. "So, maybe something slithered through here after Rayna was captured."

"No, the tracks tell me they walked upright in formation with at least two prisoners dragged along behind."

One of the Wardens chuckled. "You're saying lizard men took the girl?"

"Yes." Paz seemed unfazed even as the laughter infected the entirety of the group. "Maybe something of a hybrid. Would that be so hard to believe?"

He turned his attention to Coraise and raised an eyebrow as if to tell him it wasn't unfounded. Coraise nodded a silent agreement. Since learning about the Night Howlers and their mutation into wolves he knew anything was possible. That didn't mean he had to like it.

Coraise had dealt with warriors from all walks of life. Each time they presented new challenges but he never feared losing. All he needed was one blow to cut deep into their flesh. Once the blood flowed from their body Coraise knew he could kill whatever stood before him.

Now, with the magical creatures once again running rampant on Atharia, he didn't know whether they bled or not. That uncertainty made him uneasy. Even Rayna's dragoneye gave him chills. What could the Source Gods have been thinking to make such a rare beauty and then stick a monstrous orb inside her skull?

Or perhaps even Rayna herself came from dark magic. That would stand to reason why she traveled with a dragon. And why the king and queen seemed so adamant about retrieving both of them.

To his credit Paz hadn't given up searching. He dropped to his haunches and felt the dirt in his hands. Bringing the soft earth to his nose he inhaled so deeply Coraise thought he might taste it. Then Paz scattered the dirt out in front of him and stood.

"The ground around here is soft...too soft for this region."

He pointed out a path of ground that butted up just against the side of the Dragon's Backbone. Coraise looked to see what Paz saw but couldn't make out any difference.

"So what does that mean?"

"I believe we're dealing with a false floor."

A false floor was usually employed inside a dwelling as

an easy escape route. The town of Theopilous was ripe with them throughout its brothels. Too many times a man's wife had come looking for him as he enjoyed the pleasures of another woman. The false floors gave him a chance to get away before getting caught.

The idea made its way across Atharia into homes, taverns, and even into royal houses. It helped to have a quick way to escape from slaughter when a siege broke out. But to use the trick their needed to be floor panels to dig into and a structure atop it.

"How could there be a false floor out her in the middle of the wilderness?" Coraise asked.

"That's where the soft ground comes in."

Paz stepped over to a large clump of dirt and started shifting it around with the toe of his boot. The others watched as the dirt began to thin out and clear. Beneath the soil a wooden hatch revealed itself.

Paz smiled. "Good thing I came along."

Coraise gave him a pat on the back then his eyebrows twitched in thought. Another look at the forest flooring told him everything he needed to know. He drew his sword and motioned for the others to do the same. Paz stepped back in defense suspecting the attack was meant for him.

"Someone had to cover the hatch back over after they left," Coraise told him. "We're being watched."

As though his words summoned them, a small army of

creatures burst from the trees. They dressed in leather armor and breeches like men but their faces told another story. Short, round snouts and eyes in slits were amplified by hard scales across the skin.

Coraise did not want to be touched by such things for fear of being turned to one. He used every skill he ever learned to fend off the attackers. They were small but many and they quickly swarmed the scene going after the Righteous Wardens with overwhelming odds.

Paz got caught up in the attack as well. That is when he finally shifted. From the corner of his eye Coraise watched as dark fur covered his body and fangs drew down from his lips. He became a massive four-legged beast that could more easily rip the scaled creatures asunder.

Coraise doubled up on his swords by pulling Rayna's from his belt as well. Wish as he might he couldn't get the blade to erupt in flame. But fire would come from the sky. Propelled by the red dragon he glided down from out of nowhere.

The dragon had grown in size since Coraise saw him last. With wings outstretched he torched the scaly hides of the lizard men as he passed overhead.

Their scales acted as armor keeping them from catching fire. But it was enough of a distraction for the Righteous Wardens to sway the advantage. Coraise capitalized by lopping the heads off the two enemy who cornered him.

The red dragon provided one more pass over attack before disappearing into the trees. Coraise tried to keep eyes on the direction he headed. Wherever he traveled to, Rayna would be close by.

As he kept watch on the dragon another assailant took him by surprise. The creatures were smaller than full grown men but faster than the most. Coraise himself could move his large frame with agile steps. For all his training, he couldn't keep pace with the magical creatures.

The lizard man came for his face. Coraise turned his body in time to avoid losing an eye. Only the tip of the blade caught him across the cheek. He pivoted in his step ready to meet his attacker face-to-face. Then another leaped from the bushes onto his back. Coraise had to fend off the first one while trying to shake the other from his torso. It proved overwhelming.

They went for his knees to break his height then clawed at his face. Sometime in the chaos he lost both his swords while trying to defend his eyes and throat. The pair of creatures scrambled atop him snapping their teeth towards exposed flesh.

Coraise felt the panic set in. On his back, unarmed, and outnumbered he feared the worst. Then an unlikely ally presented himself. Paz threw himself into the fray knocking one of the creatures off with his hind feet. Then he caught the other's tail in his mouth and dragged him away too.

This gave Coraise the opening to regroup. He gathered his swords and went after the assailants with no mercy. While Paz engaged one, Coraise battled the other. Size and strength soon won out over speed and the hybrid creatures fell all around. When the dust cleared only one member of the Righteous Wardens had perished. That left them with six including Coraise and Paz who shifted back to human form.

"I owe you my life," Coraise told him. "But by the Gods man, put some clothes on."

Paz laughed. "I can't shift my clothing, only my body. It's made for some interesting predicaments"

As Paz gathered his things the Wardens approached Coraise. They had concerns about traveling with such a being as Paz. Coraise couldn't fault them for that, especially after surviving an attack from a pack of hybrids.

"What is going on with all these creatures, Coraise?" asked his lieutenant Meric Easton. "We signed up to track down an enemy to the crown and drag her back to receive justice. Magic beings were never part of the bargain. Especially to travel with one."

"Consider it an adventure," Coraise told him.

Meric shook his head. "Consider it a pay raise."

"Of course, my friend. I wouldn't expect otherwise. Now, let's discuss terms."

He wrapped his arm about Meric's shoulders and slowly led him into the brush. When he grew certain the others could not see, Coraise used Meric's own dagger to stab him multiple times starting with the throat so he couldn't scream.

Meric's body dropped into the bushes with the fallen corpses of the lizard men. Coraise wiped his hands, tossed the dagger, and returned to the rest of the Wardens with solemn news.

"I'm afraid Meric won't be continuing on with the rest of us. His cowardice overtook him and he ran back to town." Coraise shrugged then smiled. "That just means more gold to go around!"

The remaining Wardens were fine with that arrangement. But Paz and his keen sense of smell knew otherwise. He sidled up to Coraise and spoke low so the others did not hear.

"Is there a blade to the gut in my future?"

"No need to worry, Paz. As I said, I owe you."

"Then may I suggest we continue our trek and see where the false flooring leads?"

Coraise stiffened. The thought of crawling into a hole where more of the lizard creatures could be hiding concerned him. He also had to wonder why the red dragon flew freely without Rayna anywhere in sight.

"I think we should split up," he said. "I'll seek the dragon while the rest of you go into the tunnels."

Paz disagreed. "I'm not going in there without you there to keep the Wardens from killing me."

"You'll be fine."

"We had an arrangement, Coraise," Paz argued. "Besides, you're not going to find Ryu unless he wants you too."

Paz's words gave Coraise pause. He knew the dragon by name which solidified the fact that Paz spent more time with Rayna than simply as an adversary. It changed things considerably.

"Very well, but you go first."

Coraise motioned to the large hole in the ground. Paz hesitated but then agreed. The Righteous Wardens followed him in with Coraise taking up the rear as they marched towards the unknown.

15
Born of the Dragon

R ayna missed having Bhrytbyrn in hand. The heft of the blade, its durability, and of course the burst of flame that came when called all sculpted her attack style. She learned to be adept with other weapons but nothing compared to her first. She longed to be reunited with her sword and her dragon. First, she would have to dispatch the rest of the retched clan who took her from them.

Slowly she headed back down into the bowels of the Red Waste. Each step became marked with drops of her blood as she inched her way inside. Her eyes kept watch on the room as the fire pit came into view. Keeping her back flat to the wall she slid her way into the shadows and waited.

The firelight was low indicating nothing roasted over it. K'lani remained safe for the time being. The Kappa sat in small groups as they continued feasting on Gusto. It made Rayna cringe every time they bit into the horse's dead flesh.

Marching in from the right where K'lani remained chained came the leader. He stood with a posture that spoke of bravado rather than any earned respect. Rayna saw now that these Kappa shared more in common with humans than she first thought. They were arrogant and gluttonous. It would be their downfall.

"Why haven't Arnacus and Pietrie returned yet?" the leader asked with notable frustration.

"We're not sure, Kreasus," a soldier responded. "They've been gone for some time."

"Grimlo, go see what's taking so long," Kreaus ordered. "Bring Talma and Nima with you. If those two fools are defiling that human I want you to kill all three of them."

"Understood," Grimlo responded.

The Kappa stood and gathered his gear. He motioned for two others to join him as their leader requested. These two were slender and looked to be of the female persuasion. Rayna knew when they stepped outside the first thing visible was Pietrie's body. She needed a plan but her thoughts were not clear.

The trio started towards the stairs when Grimlo stopped short. He stood paces from Rayna sniffing the

air with concern. Her head grew dizzy from loss of blood.
The bite in her shoulder made it difficult to hold the
sword aloft. But despite the obstacles Rayna straightened
up and readied herself for what she must do next. Her
grip tightened on the swords as she prepared.

Talma gave Grimlo a small push to keep him moving
and he waved her away. Stepping past Rayna's hiding
spot, Grimlo hunched down and touched the ground
with his fingers. He turned and showcased fresh blood
to the females. When they noted the coloring and
freshness they too began to sniff around. It was then that
Rayna attacked.

She went for Grimlo first and lopped off his extended
arm at the elbow. He fell back wailing as his blue-black
blood sprayed against the walls and onto his
companions. The females were also taken by surprise
from the attack. Rayna swung both swords in an arc and
caught Talma across the face. Her lithe body flipped over
from the force of the blow. Nima used her tail to spring
out of the way and avoid the swords. By then, the others
inside the hovel became alerted.

Rayna counted five including the leader. It would be a
challenging fight on a normal day. Today had been
anything but normal. Her wounds were great and she
feared their numbers would overpower her waning
strength. Instead, Rayna relied on the arrogance of
Kreasus to even the odds.

"Just you," she said, pointing her sword towards him. "You and I fight for rights to the Ischon girl."

Kreasus motioned for the others to stand down. A smile twitched on Rayna's face. Now that she piqued his interest she only needed to convince him of accepting the challenge.

"What makes you think you're on the same level as The Kappa to have a claim on the girl?"

"This does."

Rayna inched forwards into the firelight where the others could see her. She pointed to her dragoneye knowing that the light of the fire glinted off it like an amethyst jewel. The Kappa hissed with a mix of fear and awe. Kreasus snarled then softened back into a scholarly countenance.

"You dismiss me as a dirty hybrid co-mingling human blood with another species," Rayna continued. "But like you I was born with this stigma. I wear it proudly as a sign of my bond with the dragons. You let Ryu go free yet you do not offer me the same respect. A mistake."

Whether he believed her or not, Rayna could see his reptile eyes scanning her. The wounds in her flesh and body hunched over with weakness made him believe she would be an easy defeat. That was his true mistake.

As expected, his arrogance overwhelmed any common sense and he accepted Rayna's challenge. The showman in Kreasus wanted to bask in the adoration of his people.

For him, it was a chance to solidify his leadership once and for all. For Rayna, it was a chance to escape with her head.

Taking on the rest of the Kappa clan would prove too difficult in her weakened condition. Dealing with just the leader would be an arduous task but she felt better about the odds. Rayna threw down a similar challenge years before in Kartha. It proved to be the only way out of an otherwise deadly situation. The same held true now.

"I take it you bested Pietrie and Arnacus?" Kreasus asked.

"If by bested you mean I slaughtered them and left their carcasses to rot in the sun, then yes."

"I'll make you pay for that."

His words were meant to inspire. The Kappa cheered for Kreasus to avenge their fallen comrades. In the corner of the room Rayna had her own cheering section. K'lani, still bound by chains against the wall, called out encouragement. Rayna gave her a nod and then put her focus on the battle at hand.

Kreasus pulled his blade from the scabbard at his belt. Then he took a second sword from one of his comrades. He slashed the air a few times to get used to the weight then smiled his wicked smile.

"You have two. Now I have two," he told her. "It's only fair."

"Fair is not having any interference from your clan,"

Rayna argued.

"Very well." Kreasus turned towards the others and issued an order. "None of you are to interfere no matter what happens."

The crowd gathered to watch their leader destroy the outsider. They didn't think he needed any help. She was the walking wounded after all. An inferior specimen to their kind. Rayna didn't care what they thought of her. All that mattered was that they had honor enough not to get involved.

Kreasus toyed with her at first. He darted into her space to lightly tap her on the arm or butt with the flat of his blade. Rayna remained in defensive posture only circling when he did. The next time Kreasus moved forward Rayna met him with her own attack.

She swung one blade across his middle while the other struck for his head. But Kreasus was ready for her. He moved with speed and precision blocking each sword with his own. Rayna could see why The Kappa named him their leader. He'd be a formidable opponent even if she were at full strength.

The next move belonged to Kreasus. He used his tail to swipe at her feet. It caused Rayna enough distraction that she took her eyes off his swords. Had K'lani not shouted out in warning the fight would've ended with Rayna impaled. But she managed to roll backwards away from the attack.

Kreasus' face grew even more monstrous with anger. He took a step backwards to slap K'lani across for costing him the victory. She covered her head as best she could expecting the beating to continue. Rayna made certain that it wouldn't.

With Kreasus putting his attention on K'lani, it gave Rayna an opening. She used what strength remained in her body to run up the crest of the wall and leap down on Kreasus.

His people shouted a warning as well but it was too late. Rayna slashed both swords down into the top of his head with all her might. The scales cracked like a coconut shell. Grayish puss and dark blood burst from the brain sack and oozed across his face.

Rayna watched the lizard eyes flicker and roll back until only the white underbelly showed. Kreasus sputtered out fragmented sentences. His arms and legs twitched a few times as though he still tried to stay in the fight. Then he fell backwards taking the swords with him in his skull.

Unarmed, shaking from pain and fatigue, Rayna faced the others prepared to take them all on with her bare hands. But they did not engage. A few of them cursed her or spat. Then they looked to their leader dead on the ground and instead of seeking revenge they decided to honor the pact.

"Take your friend and leave our dwelling," Nima told

her. "And be quick about it."

Rayna wasted no time accepting their offer. She freed K'lani from the chains and the two of them hurried from the lair. Several times Rayna checked back over her shoulder to see if The Kappa meant to attack. They no longer paid the humans any heed.

Their attention turned to their leader where they scooped him up and dumped him upon the fire. A fitting end for the way things started.

16
Power Grab

T he longer they remained beneath the surface, the more uncomfortable Coraise felt. As the tunnel went on it grew narrower making it unfavorable for combat. Worse than that, Coraise held considerable height on the creatures who built it and he was forced to hunch for the majority of the trek.

Having a decent light source also became an issue. Even with torches in hand there were still pockets of shadows running along the walls. At any moment one of those things could jump out and attack them all.

Then another problem presented itself. Movement slowed and stalled ahead. From his vantage point Coraise couldn't see the issue. Rather than call out and give away their position he asked the Warden in front of him to suss out the situation. After conversing with the two men in front, the Warden came back with an answer.

"There's some type of blockade."

"So, move it."

His orders given were not a request but a demand. However, try as they might the Wardens couldn't clear the path. Frustrated and running short on time Coraise pulled Rayna's broadsword from his belt and tried to will it to ignite. Nothing happened.

"Dog, come here."

He whistled for Paz in a manner that the man found insulting but the wolf seemed compelled to obey. Paz shuffled his way to Coraise's side and raised his eyebrows in question.

"You called me up to see you holding your sword."

"This is Rayna's sword, you fool. Tell me how to bring flames to it."

"Why would I know that?"

"Because you lay with her, wolf." The sickening thought made him spit on the ground before continuing. "I'm sure you became privy to her tricks."

"It's not a trick, Coraise. Her dragoneye summons the flame," Paz explained. "I would've expected you to remember that since you saw it up close and personal."

Coraise grumbled. "I don't like magic. Never have. We'll have to do this the old fashioned way."

He pushed his men aside and began striking the blockade with the blade. The sound of the strikes echoed through the tunnel and pierced their ears with a wail.

"You don't have the angle to cut through," Paz told him. "Stop striking so we can think of something else."

Angered, and not willing to accept defeat, Coraise felt something bubbling up from deep inside of him. An untapped rage set off like a torch to a keg of Chaos Fire.

He ducked down and tucked his arms to his chest then launched himself into the blockade. Tight as a battering ram he hit the structure once, twice more until it buckled inward. Heavy, thick chunks of wood splintered from the frame revealing a hidden door.

"They've gone to alot of trouble to keep their secrets," Coraise said through huffs of breath. "I want to see what they're hiding."

He slipped is way through the ruined door to the other side only to find more scaly monsters to contend with. They held long, curved spears that they thrust towards him. He managed to parry two and then a third came from the side.

The tip nicked him in the upper thigh causing him to collapse. Fighting from his back he tried to keep the enemy at bay while his party pushed through and engaged. The scaled creatures seemed to be everywhere all at once. They struck down with their spears trying to skewer him like a fish.

Coraise rolled and shifted until he found distance enough to spring to his feet. Fighting carried out all around him. From the corner of his eye he saw another of his Wardens fall to the beasts. Then they came for Coraise.

He pivoted to keep his back protected from attack and stumbled over chains latched to the wall. Prisoners were held there. Perhaps the shackles kept Rayna there not too long ago.

The battle pushed them farther into the room where scant light came only from a burning fire pit. A strong scent of charring permeated the room. Coraise gagged on the thick stench as he recognized it as flesh. Had they arrived too late? Did Rayna's supple, strong body roast in the pit already? His answers would have to wait until they dispatched all the creatures. It proved a more difficult task than before.

The females of the species moved with an agility that surpassed the finest warriors Coraise ever met. Only the wolfman Paz could keep up with them. He'd once again shifted to fur and fangs to overwhelm his prey.

With Rayna's broadsword stretched out in front of him, Coraise watched the battle with keen eyes. He moved in only when the right moment presented itself and struck down another scaled soldier in the process. The sword cut through the creatures with ease. On his next strike, Coraise chopped one in half.

A smile crossed his blood-stained face as he felt the power within the special blade. He needed to know more about the sword and the woman who wielded it.

Something so rare only comes into a man's life once. Coraise intended on devouring it. But, he needed one of the creatures alive to find out where they'd taken Rayna.

With the battle all but won he found his choice. Paz had a female cornered as he bared his fangs and growled at her. She shielded her face with her arm and muttered in a foreign tongue. Coraise set his hand on the coarse fur of the wolf and pushed him back. Then he kneeled before the creature and pulled away her arm so she would face him.

"Prayers?" he asked. She nodded. "Whatever gods you pray to cannot help you now. But I can. All you have to do is answer my question and I'll let you live."

Scared and outnumbered the creature took the offer. She begged for her life giving them answers to questions Coraise didn't really care about. He simply asked to engage her trust and suss out her level of truth before the real interrogation.

During his questioning they learned the things name was Nima and she was of The Kappa clan. Another human-hybrid race left over from the days when magic ruled Atharia rather than steel. The Kappa were the weaker of the magical species but they were resourceful. While the others were hunted to extinction, the Kappa moved underground. Over the years they developed a system of tunnels to move unseen from place to place. They also developed a taste for human flesh.

"Is that why you took the girl?"

The creatures eyes flashed to slits then softened. With the remaining Wardens and a massive wolf surrounding her there wasn't much she could do but answer or die. So, Coraise asked again.

"A muscular blonde with a bejeweled eye and a baby dragon. Where did you take her?"

"That one is cursed, damned. I told Kreasus not to take her but he did not heed my warning."

"Who is Kreasus?"

"Our leader. He's dead now." Nima motioned to the fire pit. "Your woman killed him."

Coraise felt a flutter of relief in his chest. "The woman still lives then?"

"She's wounded. Not sure how long she will last."

As Nima spoke of Rayna's plight it was then that Paz turned back to his human form. He pushed past Coraise to ask questions of his own; questions that revealed what Coraise already knew to be true. Paz didn't trail Rayna for revenge. He cared for her.

"Where did she go?" Paz asked, his voice a mix of ache and fear. "You must tell me so I may help her."

Nima pointed past the fire pit to a long set of stone steps. With the chaos of battled simmered, Coraise now saw a fight already raged here. Bodies were littered by the steps, dispatched with a fury only Rayna could embody. A twitch of a smile crossed his lips.

"You've done well," he told Nima.

"I may go now?"

Her voice was weak and small as she asked permission to live. Something about her tone aroused him. Had she been human he may have indulged himself. But the sight of the scales and the snout were vile. Still, Coraise would have his fun.

"Of course, I'm a man of my word."

He motioned towards the tunnels they previously breached and allowed her to walk out. Nima moved with caution and kept looking back in anticipation of attack. Once she reached the entry to the tunnel Coraise saw the relief come and the tightness left her shoulders. That's when he motioned to his men. The remaining Wardens struck Nima down with an unmatched aggression. Her screams echoed off the walls of the dreary cavern until finally stopping in a blood-curdling hiss.

"What're you doing?" Paz asked, daring to grab Coraise by the shoulder. "You said she could leave. You said you were a man of your word."

Coraise looked at the dirty hand touching his skin and saw only a paw. His eyes clicked over to Paz's own full of remorse for the fallen enemy. Pity was a weakness that Coraise despised. He twisted into Paz's grip and whispered to him.

"I lied."

Before Paz realized Coraise lied about a great many things it was too late. He thrust the blade of his new prize possession up into the man's belly. As Paz registered the sword penetrating his flesh anguish twisted his face into a snarl. Faster than Coraise realized was possible the man turned to wolf and bit at him. It caused Coraise to tumble backwards or else lose a part of his cheek.

The black wolf did not stay to fight. With blood dripping from his belly he charged towards the stone steps with great speed. The Wardens hurried over and pulled Coraise to his feet. He turned to the remaining three men and issued another command to sate their blood thirst.

"Hunt down that dog and bring me his hide!"

They went after the wolf shouting their sadistic intentions. Coraise followed close behind with his bloody broadsword in hand. His only intention was to finish gutting the beast and wear him like a cloak.

17
Flight of the Dragon

With K'lani on her arm they fled from their captors and didn't stop running until the bodies Rayna dropped were specks in the distance. She lasted another mile across the scorching sands of the Red Waste before fatigue and her wounds over took her.

K'lani tried but failed to carry her weight and ended up dropping Rayna. The soft sand broke her fall but still stung the flesh of her face. She rolled over trying to relieve the burn only to have her back and buttocks take it instead.

Her entire body was racked with pain. Soon she would succumb to her wounds. Try as she might K'lani couldn't get Rayna back to her feet. The girl tried to pull and push with all her might but to no avail. Finally, she started to yell orders.

"You have to get up, Rayna. We have to keep moving!"

Rayna struggled to sit up. The wound in her side screamed each time the muscles flexed in movement. She propped herself up on her good arm while trying to shield the fierce sun from her eyes with the other. Her voice like gravel she told K'lani to leave her and go. The girl would hear none of it.

Squatting low she tried again to lift Rayna up. She heard K'lani whispering something of a prayer to one of the Source Gods. A sudden rush of wind at her back seemed to propel them both making it easier for K'lani to carry her. They only made it a few more paces before coming to another stop. This time they were fortunate enough to find a bit of shelter.

Remnants of a once great city sat in ruin half-buried beneath the unyielding desert. The fallen towers were enough to shield them from the rays of the sun pressing down. Rayna felt herself slipping into unconsciousness. Her body lost too much blood and now sweat expelled from her skin as well. She felt like a withering corpse that didn't quite realize it was dead.

K'lani hovered over her trying to staunch her wounds and keep her conscious. She asked questions and forced Rayna to answer them. At first they were innocent enough. K'lani asked Rayna about her travels and if she'd ever been to Ischon. Then they grew personal.

"Your eye. It's...special to say the least. How did you

get it."

"I am cursed," Rayna told her. "One more reason why you shouldn't be traveling with me."

"I don't think it's a curse. I think it's beautiful. Reminds me of my sister Kemi's jeweled necklaces. She often received jewels as gifts from her suitors."

With the topic of her sister now open, K'lani steered into treacherous waters. She asked about her sister Kemi's intended husband and his whereabouts. It seemed the truth of her travels to Atharia were to find this man.

"He goes by the name Valerios, have you seen him?"

"Yes, I know Valerios," Rayna muttered.

K'lani pressed her with more questions. "Do you know where I can find him? He was supposed to return to Kemi and has not been heard from."

"He's dead."

The words slipped from Rayna's dry lips before she realized what she said. Her reveal of the truth staggered K'lani and she stepped back leaving Rayna's wounds exposed.

Rayna forced open her eyes and tried to read K'lani's face. Her emotions were a twisted mix of anger and anguish. She paced a line in the hot sand trying to force back her hurt. It didn't work. With fresh tears streaming down her cheeks she turned back to Rayna and asked a question painful for both of them.

"Did you kill him?"

Rayna slowly shook her head. "I did not. But I am responsible for his death."

"How so?" K'lani asked, wiping the tears away with the back of her hand.

Before Rayna could answer her she spotted something traveling towards them. It moved fast but staggered rather than moving in a straight line. She motioned for K'lani to hide. As the girl ducked for cover behind a cracked spire Rayna dug herself into the sand hoping it would be enough.

Fading in and out of consciousness she tried to keep eyes on the intruder. At first she could not tell whether it were man or beast and then she realized it was both. A massive wolf with dark fur trotted up just paces away. It sniffed the air and let out a howl. The guttural sound turned to the anguished calls of Damaris de Paz as he cried out for Rayna.

The sight of him standing naked screaming her name in the middle of the Red Waste snapped Rayna awake. But she did not move right away. Perhaps the desert played tricks on her mind and this was but an illusion. Only when she saw the fresh blood running down his belly did Rayna know he was real.

Anger and love battled each other to win Rayna's heart. Paz had betrayed her and stole off with Ryu only to succumb to dragon's fire from the mighty Nazalon. Or

that's what she thought happened. Now here he stood
wounded by blade shouting for Rayna. Her heart won
over her head and she went to him.

Pushing free from the sand she crawled out from
hiding. When Paz saw her emerge his eyes filled with
tears and he fell to his knees. Rayna made it to him just
before his head hit the sand. She caught him by the
shoulders and cradled his wounded body against her
own. Seeing the reunion, K'lani came out from behind
the spire.

"Who is this?" she asked.

Rayna waved her off. Now was not the time. Paz was
trying to tell her something but the blood filling his
lungs made it difficult to speak. She leaned down closer
to catch his whisper on her ear.

"I'm sorry for everything," he said. "But now you must
run!"

The words were given on his last breath with as much
insistence as he could shout them. As the life left his
body Rayna felt an ache pierce her heart like an arrow.
She pressed her lips to his forehead and held him until
K'lani made an unsettling observation.

"Someone is coming!"

Setting Paz down gently upon the sand Rayna found
the strength to stand. She looked out towards the
horizon from whence they had come and saw shapes in
the distance. They did not move with the same speed as

the wolf but they were sure footed.

"The Kappa?" K'lani asked, fear cracking her voice.

Rayna didn't like the answer but she knew of no others who would be coming for them. Paz must've been tracking her since she thought he burned in the fire. His wounds surely came at the hands of the Kappa. Now they approached to claim the woman who slayed their leader. Letting them leave the chamber was a ruse.

They knew that two human girls wouldn't last long in the Red Waste. Their reptilian hides could thwart the scorching sun long enough to drag their prey back beneath the earth. Wounded, unarmed, and outnumbered they would be taken and eaten by the Kappa.

Then Rayna saw a shadow cast down across the sands. One minute the skies were calm, the next came a beautiful vision on crimson wings. Ryu circled overhead a moment then swooped down suddenly. He landed in front of them screeching loud as though he gave a dire warning. Both relieved and impressed Rayna fell into him and hugged her dragon around the neck.

"Can he fly us out of here?" K'lani was desperate to escape.

Rayna shook her head. "Not both of us."

Ryu grew fast as was the nature of a dragon. But he was still too small to support so much weight upon him. Perhaps if the Kappa saw he was their ally they would

back off in their attack. But as the group grew closer
Rayna saw it wasn't the Kappa who came for them after
all. Coraise Kennethgorian and the Righteous Wardens
raced across the sand with death on their minds. Death
for all who opposed them.

18
Dragon Defender

T his time when Rayna told K'lani to leave her she insisted upon it. She would not let Ryu be taken by the mercenaries. And though both the young girl and small dragon wanted to stay and fight Rayna ordered them to go.

She stooped down and set her hand upon Ryu's head. He bowed solemnly as though he knew what she was willing to do. Then she turned to K'lani whose eyes registered the same emotion.

"I need you to be strong and swift," Rayna told her.

Behind them the Righteous Wardens grew closer. Ryu set forth a blast of flame across the desert sands that would hold them but only for the moment. K'lani was fighting back a fit of tears. Rayna shook her by the shoulders and then found herself pleading.

"Please, I made a vow to keep him safe." Her voice

cracked under the weight of emotion. "It's up to you now. Go!"

She physically led K'lani over to Ryu and implored her again to leave. This time, the girl listened. She straightened herself up and sought Ryu's permission to sit atop him. Rayna feared the weight would be too much. But her dragon companion had proven to be resilient in many ways during their journey. This time was no different.

Ryu began a slow trot then spread wide his wings before pressing up into the sky. K'lani clung to his neck with her eyes closed murmuring a chant or prayer of some sort. Rayna watched with anticipation from below as the two of them soared away. Once her companions were no longer in danger she turned her attention to the oncoming lot.

~

When Coraise saw Rayna standing there, covered in sand and dried blood, he licked his lips. To her credit she smiled back at him. Whatever harrowing escapades she'd been through hadn't dampened her spirit. He liked that. Made it more challenging.

Off to the side Paz lay in a crumpled mess. A pool of blood dried beneath his lifeless body. Coraise motioned with his head and gave a wide, toothy grin.

"I did that."

This time Rayna did not appease him with more bravado. Paz's death truly irked her.

"You're going to pay for it."

Her threat made Coraise revel in his actions even more. There was something deliciously intoxicating about instilling pain in others. It aroused him to the highest of levels.

"Looks like those disgusting creatures almost got the better of you," he told her. "You'll be no match for me."

"I've bested you twice before, Coraise. I can do it again."

"Rayna, you're unarmed, half-dead, and your dragon just flew away. Don't be foolish. Just give up."

"I may have done some horrible things in my past but I've never given up."

She moved towards the lot of them intent on going out swinging. Coraise intended on bringing her back alive. But that didn't mean he couldn't have his fun first. He motioned his Wardens to initiate the attack.

As they moved towards her, Rayna managed to knock one of his Wardens unconscious. He dropped face first into the sand. The weight of him caused the dust to bounce up and sting at the eyes. Coraise stepped back to clear his vision only to find Rayna running up on him next.

~

Rayna knew she would die there that day. A pity to go out in the Red Waste. Soon the tale would be that the sands swallowed her whole like so many other unsuspecting travelers. But she didn't care much for her legend.

Her concern lay with Ryu and whether K'lani could take care of him. If by some twisted chance of fate she made it out alive she would spend the last of her days trying to find them.

Coraise didn't expect Rayna to charge him. His ego developed over the years from taking out high-profile targets. A man with his height and skill with a sword knew how to use both. But now that Rayna was upon him she realized it was her sword not his that Coraise swung around. If she could get her hands back on Bhrytbyrn the odds would shift back in her favor.

~

Coraise saw Rayna recognize her sword. He watched her strange, dark eye covet the blade as he held it. Up close the iris shone a like an amethyst jewel while the slit of a pupil locked on the sword. It unnerved Coraise to the point in which he tossed the sword away. Better to lose one blade than have it ignite in his hands.

As he tossed it to the ground Rayna made a desperate lunge to grab it. Coraise let her take it and led her to believe she had a fighting chance. But as she grasped the hilt he came in from behind her and slashed the back of her thigh with his own sword.

She buckled and dropped the broadsword. Her hand twisting back to touch the fresh wound. Coraise kicked the back of her other knee and knocked her to the ground. She scrambled to get up but was drained from the sun and her wounds. Coraise felt pity for her until she threw sand in his face.

He turned his head in time to shield his eyes but Rayna was already on the move. She grabbed his sword arm struggling to free the blade from his grip. The wounds in her flesh had not diminished her strength.

Her strong arms wrenched against his own. She would not falter and it began to frustrate Coraise. He knew his fun was over so he ended the fight. Driving his knee up into her lacerated stomach it doubled her over. She fell to the ground gasping for air and spitting blood across the sand. Still, she would not quit.

As she looked up at him with that strange eye it made Coraise feel frightened for the first time. His discomfort switched to a deep, bubbling rage that he unleashed through his fist. Striking Rayna across the jaw he knocked her unconscious and finally closed the eye.

"No wonder she wears that eye patch," he muttered. Then he turned to his Wardens. "None of you thought to step in and help me?"

"We were too busy enjoying the show," one man chuckled.

Coraise laughed with him. Then he picked up Rayna's sword from the ground and cut off the man's head with it. Only one of the Wardens remained standing. He was slender with a youthful appearance that told Coraise he'd not been in many battles.

"Do you want to test me as well?" Coraise asked him.

The boy shook his head and took a few steps back. Coraise halted him before he ran off shrieking through the sands only to be swallowed by the Red Waste. He pointed to the man Rayna knocked unconscious and instructed the boy to rouse him.

"Wake that one and let us be on our way," he said. "I want to get this stinking desert off me."

They would travel back through the underground passageway. The last two Wardens in Coraise's service carried Rayna while he led the way. He kept his eyes peeled for more creatures, more magic, or the return of the dragon.

19
Deal for the Dragon

F alkon walked the floor of the throne room like a caged animal. He tried to sit several times but the anticipation proved too great. Nadiuska and the Daughters of Chaos chose not to be present for the event.

"This is your moment. Enjoy it," Nadiuska had told him. "Then afterwards enjoy your spoils."

With that she kissed her king rousing him to the heightened state he was in now. It was better that his queen would not be there. He intended to do such things to the dragonslayer that a woman should not see.

It seemed like an eternity since the guards at the gate let Coraise and his men pass. Then the large chamber doors pushed open and they were there. Finally, the moment he'd been waiting for since their encounter on the Graven Peaks had arrived. He would face Rayna the Dragonslayer once again.

However, when they entered the throne room he did not see the mighty warrior woman he knew her to be. Instead, the Righteous Wardens dragged a disheveled, broken mess into the room. Coraise took Rayna the rest of the way up the dais and threw her at Falkon's feet.

He looked down at the battered woman in front of him and for a moment thought Coraise might be trying to trick him. Squatting down he dared to take her chin in his hands and look her over. The woman's hands were bound in heavy chain keeping her from attacking. Not that she would fair well considering the battle wounds upon her shoulder and torso.

She tried to pull her head free of Falkon's grip and he snatched her dirty, blonde locks to control her. Then he saw the strange eye staring back at him like a portal to another realm. A smile crossed his lips as he confirmed the woman was indeed Rayna. She scowled back at him; a look he'd seen more than once in their dealings.

Falkon stood and brushed his hands off on the length of his robe. She was filthy and held the stink of a hog pen. Still, he had the dragonslayer at his mercy.

"You couldn't have left some fun for me, Coraise?" he asked motioning to Rayna's wounds.

"Your order said to bring her back. It never said she had to be in pristine condition," Coraise argued.

"I suppose it will do. Truth be told I didn't even think you would get the job done."

"Yet I did and I want my earnings for it. We all do."

He motioned over his shoulder to the two men at his flank. They looked like a father and son duo recently plucked off a farm. Neither appeared very formidable. Falkon grew curious of the tale on how this rag-tag band captured the mighty slayer.

"You'll have all that's owed you and more," he said, slapping his hands together. "We'll commence a veritable feast in your honor."

No doubt ravenous from their journey the men were quick to agree to terms. Mercenaries always succumb to the mention of a good meal and a warm bath. Falkon even promised to provide them women for their reward as well.

Then he turned his attentions back to Rayna. She had not tried to fight her way out or even to move from where Coraise dropped her. Falkon was disappointed. Instead of the cocky warrior with the smart mouth he got a shell of her former self. He wanted to crush her spirit and break her will. In her present state it would be meaningless.

"I owe you pain," he told her.

"And I owe you a blade to the gut...for Valerios!"

Her bravado returned to her with fresh venom on her words. Having Valerios' name brought up angered Falkon. The reason for his friend's death sat in front of him spewing toxic tales of revenge fantasies. The king would not be insulted in his own house.

"No, my dear, I owe you for Valerios."

With that he slapped her across the face causing her to fall over. Coraise reached down and pulled her back up tearing part of her jerkin in the process. Falkon looked over her body, a once powerful sight, now stained with blood and grime. Her shoulders slumped and she could hardly keep her head up.

"Guards, take this filth to the dungeon," he ordered. "I tire of looking at her."

Two of the guards dragged Rayna from his sight though she did not go willingly. Beaten and bloodied she still struggled against their grip until a third man joined to overpower her legs.

Falkon couldn't help but smile. "There's that fiery spirit! Half-dead and she still tries to escape."

"Yes, she's a spitfire," Coraise agreed. "She made it deep into the Red Waste with no flagon or food."

The mention of the scorching desert made Falkon cringe. "I traveled out that way the first time we sought the warrior woman on my father's order. I hate that place. Nothing but sand and shit for miles."

"Not true," Coraise said, helping himself to a goblet of wine. "There are creatures dwelling beneath the sands. Hideous mixed man-beasts that I've never run across before."

"One more reason not to venture there again."

Falkon poured his own goblet then waited for Coraise to speak his needs. He'd made himself comfortable in one of the large chairs down by the dining tables. His feet were kicked up on another chair tracking mud across the fine satin cushions.

"Is there a reason you're still here in my presence?" Falkon asked.

"I'm awaiting my reward," Coraise reminded him. "You know, the one scrawled upon the bounties littered across this land."

"I said you'd be rewarded at the banquet this evening."

"I'd rather take my earnings now and be on my way." Coraise finished his wine and stood. "No offense, majesty, but something about this castle puts me on edge. As if there are spirits roaming the halls seeking new bodies to possess."

At his words the candelabras swayed overhead. The flames flickered as though a strong wind passed through the chamber. Then from the king's private entrance Nadiuska presented herself.

Her sudden appearance made Coraise take a step back. His face no longer held his usual smirk. The Righteous Wardens behind him also looked unnerved by the presence of the queen. But how could a lithe, supple beauty cause grown men such fear? That Falkon could not discern.

He took her by the hand and led her to the throne at his

side. Then the two of them sat, king and queen of the land, looking down at their inferiors. Nadiuska was short on pleasantries. She got right to the heart of the matter, one that disturbed her verily.

"Where is the dragon?"she asked Coraise.

"You required the girl," he replied. "No deal was made for her pet."

A scowl crossed Nadiuska's face as she regarded Falkon. Darkness ebbed from her eyes and sucked him inside of them. Suddenly, he felt himself plummeting down the side of the Graven Peaks only to come to an abrupt stop at the foot of his throne. Uncertain what happened he looked over to Nadiuska who stared down at him. Her eyes soft; lips parted with concern.

"Are you alright, my love?"

Falkon took a moment to assess himself. In his mind he felt as though he plummeted from the cliffs. But his body never left the throne room. When he looked towards Coraise he expected to see the mercenary laughing. Instead, the man they said was unshakable looked scared.

"I'm fine," Falkon said as he returned to his throne. "Must've been too much wine."

Nadiuska took his hand in hers and caressed it. "Coraise says he was unaware of the deal for the dragon. Did you not relate this request to him before he departed?"

As she spoke the grip on Falkon's hand intensified until it felt as though the skin split and the bones shattered. He looked to her face to plead her to stop. Again she held the darkness in her eyes and a macabre scowl spread her full red lips.

"An oversight, my queen," Falkon said weakly. Then quieter still: "I beg you release me and I shall see the matter taken care of."

"No," Nadiuska told him. "You've already done enough."

She gave one final squeeze to his hand inflicting so much pain he felt it had been torn free. Then she went for Coraise. He stood his ground but Falkon noted his hand fall upon the broadsword tucked into his belt. Nadiuska saw as well.

"A beautiful sword, may I see it?" she asked.

Coraise didn't hesitate to appease her. "A gift to you, my queen, to make up for my error in not retrieving the dragon."

"Oh, you'll still make up for that. But first I shall provide you the means to find him."

Nadiuska took the broadsword from him in both hands and held it in front of her as though cradling a child. She did not return it to Coraise. Instead, she pushed back her robes of eminence to reveal a sheath at her back Falkon hadn't noticed before. There the broadsword rested snugly as though it had always been hers.

"Enjoy your party, Coraise Kennethgorian," she said. "You and your Wardens are welcome here as our guests. In the morning, we'll discuss dealing with the dragon. In the meantime, I'd like to see the slayer."

20
Strangers in the Night

On the journey from the Red Waste to Sandhal they provided little sustenance for Rayna. Coraise let her have just enough to eat and drink to keep her alive. They crudely patched her wounds but did not provide for much else. She could almost feel the infection swimming in her skin where the Kappa bit her.

Sickened and weak she still wouldn't let the smug Falkon feel as though he broke her. It was all she had left in her to try and fight the guards off. Now she was at their mercy as they dragged her to the holding cells in the bowels of the castle.

They removed her chains but relief lasted briefly. A new set of shackles running from the wall bound both arms. Her feet remained free but they took her boots. The men mocked her weakness and spat at her before they left.

She was fortunate that's all they did though she expected King Falkon gave strict orders on such matters. More than likely he wanted to take her himself if he could find a potion strong enough to stay erect throughout.

Rayna pulled against her bonds though she knew the attempt to be futile. The king had her. She would be his plaything until he saw fit to end her life. Such thoughts made her heart anxious with dread until she found her breathing out of control.

"Steady yourself," a voice called from the darkness. "You're having a panic attack. Take a few deep breaths and it shall pass."

She did as the stranger suggested and after a few breaths her heart stopped racing. Looking out across the cells it proved difficult to see anything other than shadow and stone. Rayna called out to offer her thanks.

"I appreciate the tip," she said. "Who are you?"

The voice spoke again from the darkness. "Just a man who has lost his way."

His tone sounded familiar to Rayna. She scooted as far inward as the chains would allow trying to hear clearer.

"How did you wind up here?"

"I crossed Captain Falkon."

"You mean King Falkon."

"Not my king."

"Nor mine."

"He was a captain of the guards when I came across his path in the Fickle Forest."

That's when Rayna placed the voice. She could scarcely believe it to be true after so much time apart. Hoping some fever from the infection wasn't causing a delusion she dared speak his name.

"Jagger?"

It was quiet for a moment then Rayna heard the scraping of chains across the ground. Moving into the bit of torchlight that shone from the wall Rayna saw him. The light fell across his blue eyes causing them to sparkle like jewels. Dusty blonde hair fell down around his ears. He picked up a new scar across his chin that looked like the blade of a sword caught him. Still, she saw the Jagger she'd known so many years before. Though weak and disheveled, he recognized her as well.

"Rayna! By the Gods is it really you?"

"I'm afraid so," she replied, embarrassed to be in such condition before him. "It's good to see you, Jagger."

"Good to see you as well though not under these conditions."

"Last we spoke I left you in Fickle Forest to run your scams on the unsuspecting travelers. What happened?"

"Seems Captain Falkon didn't take too kindly to our attempted extortion of him in the Fickle Forest that time. Shortly after you and I parted company about a dozen of his men tracked us down. They killed most of my companions, the others joined his ranks...traitorous bastards. Then they threw me in this dank cell to rot away the rest of my days. What about you? How did you end up in here?"

"I saved a dragon."

Jagger's laugh echoed over the cell block.

"No really, what do they have you on?"

"That's the truth of the matter. The other truth is that I need to get out of here before any harm comes to him."

"I've never known you to lie," Jagger said. "So you must be speaking true now. But how does a slayer of dragons come to befriend one?"

"A long story."

Jagger lifted his chains. "I'm not going anywhere. Indulge me."

Rayna gave a laugh, surprised she could still find humor under the circumstances. Then she told Jagger her tale. He listened intently about how the former king sought her to fulfill a quest. Her friendship with Valerios and Falkon's growing deceit.

She spoke on encountering a Shadax monster in the Shadowed Highlands. Then how they climbed the Graven Peaks to where she thought the enemy she tracked for years awaited her. Instead, she found the dragon Saarath and it's baby whom Rayna would later come to name Ryu.

"A dragon didn't burn my home and kill my family," she explained. "The first half of my life was a lie."

"Not all of it."

Jagger reached as far as his chains would allow. He managed to caress Rayna's finger tips with his own. Memories from the first time they touched resurfaced. She felt like a young girl fumbling her way through life again.

"You look beautiful," Jagger said.

"You lie."

"Yes," he admitted with a laugh. "You're a mess but I'm still happy to see you. It's been too long since we shared a moment."

Rayna pulled her hand away. "I need to get free of this place, Jagger. I will not be held captive while my dragon is still in danger."

"I've heard you speak this way in the past but never in the defence of a dragon."

"I made a pact to keep him safe from harm."

"You owe someone so much that you would throw away everything that made you who you are today?"

She locked eyes with him and held his gaze. "Not everything."

"If the dragons are not responsible for the death of your family then who is?" Jagger asked.

"A witch. One who toys with my life even still," she explained. "She seeks Ryu and I cannot let her lay claim to him."

"They say a witch roams the halls of the castle," Jagger said leaning against the wall. "I've heard the guards talking about many peculiar happenings late at night. Blood rituals and such."

"I should like to meet this witch."

"Be careful what you wish for."

Rayna thought Jagger joked with her but she saw he was serious. Jagger never did care for magic. He preferred the swing of a sword to sorcery. A trait passed down from his father Darius the Dreaded. It was one of the ways Rayna bonded with him in the past.

She learned at the foot of Darius as well. Strange circumstances brought her into his mixed band of mercenaries the Forsaken Force. Rayna learned much of her craft there when she became one of them. Now strange circumstances brought Jagger back into her life. She wasn't about to leave him behind.

"We need to find a way out of here."

Jagger set a finger to his lips to quiet her then pointed to the door. The guards were on the move. Four of them came down the corridor while another two watched the door. They held short swords at the ready as they approached.

A pair of them set the tips of their swords towards Jagger as a warning not to move. The other two gathered Rayna. They moved swiftly and with precision.

Apparently the king summoned the slayer and they weren't taking any chances of her escaping.

As they led her out she could hear Jagger calling for her to 'stay strong.' Rayna had every intention of remaining stoic in the face of whatever vile form of humiliation King Falkon had waiting. She would bide her time and keep him thinking he held the upper hand. Once the opening presented itself, Rayna would kill the king.

21
Dragon Queen

The guards marched Rayna on a path that looped behind Cragstone Keep where the soldiers' corridors were. She remembered the last time visiting Saltwood Stronghold. Back then the king himself summoned her as an invited guest to the castle. King Favian welcomed her with fancy clothes, a perfumed bath, and a private chamber to relax in. She was treated like royalty.

This time the king kept her out of sight stuck in a dank cell. His guards dragged her with force and spoke to her with disdain. They all thought she'd killed Valerios the Valiant. To them, she was the enemy and would be treated as such.

She was brought to a small room just off the gardens. Inside looked like a butcher's workspace and smelled just the same. Blood stained the floor and permeated the air with its strong iron stench.

A stone pulpit sat in the middle of the room. Circled around it strange carvings were etched into the floor. Rayna could not read the archaic language but she recognized the set-up as a sacrificial alter.

This new bit of information made her balk on the original plan set forth in her mind. It had been said by Valerios and others that King Favian dealt in dark magic. From the looks of things his son did as well. If Falkon meant to use magic as a means of breaking her spirit, Rayna wouldn't wait to strike.

To her chagrin, the Saltwood Soldiers overpowered her. They sat her in front of the pulpit and chained her hands to the ground. On her knees, hands stretched out in front, it appeared as though Rayna were praying to a dark lord she knew nothing about. The thought of such things frightened her and she began to shout at the soldiers to set her free.

They ignored her demands and stepped outside. The heavy wooden door shut behind them with a slam leaving Rayna alone in the strange room. She pulled at her bonds to no avail. The length of chain ran into the ground allowing for little to no movement.

If she believed the Source Gods would come she'd have asked for their help. But in all her days traveling Rayna learned enough to know the Gods did not care for the humans who roamed the world. She preferred to rely on her own wits and skills. At the moment they seemed to have led her astray.

The sound of the heavy wooden door scraping open sent a chill down her spine. She grit her teeth and prepared for what may come. A figure paced the floor behind her. No doubt Falkon looked over his prey reveling in the moment. Or perhaps Coraise snuck in to get a taste before the king.

"Come and face me, coward!" Rayna hollered.

It didn't take long for the reveal. Long dark robes with a hint of indigo laced throughout dragged across the floor. Rayna craned her neck up to see her visitor and found not whom she expected.

A woman stood before her with a pale complexion that contrasted against the dark essence of the room. Her long black hair was pushed back over her shoulders and mingled with the palatinate coloring of the robe.

Her lips sparkled like the elaborate gems that adorned her neck and fingers. Within her hands she carried Rayna's own sword Bhrytbyrn. The weapon seemed out of place in the care of such an ethereal beauty. But Rayna knew firsthand that looks could be deceiving.

"Do you know who I am, girl?" the stranger asked.

"The woman who would be queen," Rayna replied.

"I am queen. Queen Nadiuska."

"Not my queen."

"Of course. You have a warrior's heart. You live free in

the world and owe allegiance to no one. Is that right?"

Rayna hesitated with her answer as she tried to place where she'd seen the woman before. An air of familiarity emanated from Nadiuska but Rayna did not know why she felt this way. She regarded the queen with a stone jaw and replied.

"That's correct. I keep my own counsel, set my own course."

"You hesitated in your reply. Is that because you don't truly believe these things you speak?"

"I don't bend the knee to anyone willingly," Rayna told her. "The only reason I bow before you now is the chains hold me still."

Nadiuska leaned back against the stone pulpit looking down at Rayna. She enjoyed making others beg for their lives. Most rulers did. Having the chains fastened to the floor in such a manner let her tower over even the mightiest of prisoners. Why the blood stained the room was another matter and one Rayna did not wish to learn.

"Isn't it true that you owe allegiance to a dragon?"

Her words caught Rayna off guard. She didn't know how to respond without stumbling into whatever trap Nadiuska was laying.

"I made a vow to act as a protector," she explained.

"To whom did you make this vow?"

"A dragon," Rayna admitted.

"Then you do owe them allegiance."

"You twist my words, witch."

Nadiuska set the flat of the sword's blade under Rayna's chin and lifted her head up. Her piercing gray eyes almost appeared completely white from Rayna's vantage point. She stared with a hard gaze though her lips curved in a smile.

"So, you do know me."

"Yes, I recall your name now," Rayna said. "They speak of a powerful witch in the early days of Atharia who created the first flame. Intent on harvesting the power from the magical creatures who ruled the land, Nadiuska and her Daughters of Chaos challenged the ancient dragons. You lost."

"Did I? Or did I bide my time these many years using a puppet to do my bidding until my strength returned to me?"

Suddenly, Rayna's dragoneye quaked in its socket. She saw flashes of visions race across her mind from years before. Memories of seeking and slaying different dragons all across the land played out in her thoughts. She pulled away from Nadiuska's stare so fast she cut her chin on Bhrytbyrn.

"You're responsible for this curse I've been saddled with my entire life," she said through gritted teeth. "You're the witch I've been seeking. The one I'm going to kill!"

"Come now, enough of all that," Nadiuska warned her.

"You're a beaten and bloody mess chained to the floor. While I admire the bravado you're hardly in a position to speak in such a manner."

"I'll find my way free and then I'll find a way to kill you."

"I would believe that if you hadn't gone soft on me by sparing that baby dragon. It surprises me how guilt can overpower your lineage in such a way that it alters one's entire sense of purpose. Personally, I've always considered guilt a useless emotion."

"What do you mean my lineage? Are you referring to humans?"

"I'm quite human, my dear. Just a far superior specimen than the likes of you."

"Then why send me to do your bidding as you said?"

"I don't like getting my hands dirty. Besides, your father worked for me. I thought I'd keep it in the family. That curse you speak of was my gift to you along with this blood blade." She tapped the sword against her open palm. "Impressive work with the Sword of Sight but you have no idea of its true power. Shall I show you? It's the least I can do before you die."

Nadiuska set the blade aside just out of Rayna's reach. Then she came for her; a dark visage of hate and madness masked her face. She did not even touch Rayna and pain began to ebb throughout her entire being. At once she felt renewed cuts in her flesh from the Kappa attack. An old burn scar from the hands of her first dragon kill lit up on her skin as though freshly burned.

These were the tricks of dark magic that Rayna always feared. The ability to make one feel the pain from their past as if it were happening in the here and now. But Nadiuska wasn't content with reopening old wounds. She wanted to instill her own. A memorable mark upon Rayna's flesh that she would never forget.

With Rayna weakened and writhing from pain Nadiuska took hold of her face. She held Rayna's jaw with such force it felt as though her teeth would crack. Then Nadiuska reached towards her dragoneye. Her long, bejeweled fingers beckoned the eye as though it were a pet.

Rayna felt the blood vessels deep in the socket ripping free from the vitreous body. The sclera and muscles ruptured as the orb began to exit its fleshy home. Nadiuska didn't even have to touch the eye to rip it free. She simply motioned it forwards and the eye obeyed its master.

The warmth of her own blood splashed against Rayna's cheek and into her mouth as she screamed. Times before in her past she underwent torture and always managed to remain stoic no matter the pain. Rayna never wanted to let her enemy have the satisfaction of hearing her cry out.

But as her dragoneye was aggressively yanked from its

socket the pitch of her scream rattled the walls. Rayna did not care. The organ being torn from her skull is the only thing that registered around her. Everything else fell away. Soon her screams sounded like someone elses. Rayna's mind grew numb shutting itself off from the atrocity of her attack.

Once Nadiuska freed the eye entirely, Rayna's body slumped over in a state of shock. The blood continued to drip down from the vacant hole in her face and coagulate upon the floor in clumps of viscera. Nadiuska continued to speak though Rayna only heard bits and pieces of her confession.

"This is the all-seeing eye. You weren't cursed with it, you were charmed," she began. "I honored you with the gift of sight allowing you to succeed where I couldn't and killing in my honor. I watched your every move through this beautiful gift and guided you when you needed it. Together, we would've slain every dragon on Atharia and beyond.

But then you started covering up with that damned patch as though my gift was an embarrassment. You wore that patch for so long I lost track of you and it made me have to improvise with the elderly king and his fool son.

Now here you are, my long lost child, and I have you back. But since you've decided to stop slaying dragons I no longer have any use for you. So, I'm taking back my gifts. Both of them."

Through her remaining eye, Rayna watched as Nadiuska pressed the dragoneye into the hilt of Bhrytbyrn. It only took a quick flash of her hand to embed the dragon jewel within the sword as though it had been forged that way.

"Now I have the gift of sight with me for all eternity," Nadiuska said holding the sword high in the air. "It's a cruel sword and the forging of it is just as cruel. I shall dub it Blahkbyrn. A much better name, don't you think?"

She looked over at Rayna for her approval or to mock her in victory. Rayna felt herself slipping from this world into the next. Soon she would be free of all her pain. But Nadiuska wouldn't allow it.

"Blast, I know the king will pitch a fit if I let you die before he can parade you out in front of the peasants."

With that Nadiuska lit the sword. The flames upon the blade rose in a strange colored mix of deep purples and turquoise blue. She turned towards Rayna who lay on her side with blood still spilling down her face.

"Try to relax," Nadiuska said with a smile. "This is going to hurt."

As the flaming blade was placed upon her eye socket the searing of flesh brought Rayna back from the brink of death. She tried to draw away from the sword so hard the chains bit into her wrists until they bled. Nadiuska pulled the sword back and extinguished its new magical flame.

"All you had to do was bring me the blood of the baby dragon," she explained. "The sword would've stored it for you. Then we could've avoided all this unpleasantness. Now I'll find him myself and you'll die for your betrayal of the cause."

Nadiuska tapped the dragoneye blade in her palm once more then set it within a sheath at her back. She pushed open the heavy door and began speaking with the guards outside.

Rayna maintained her gaze upon the witch until the moment she left. Once Nadiuska stepped out, Rayna crumpled into a broken shell of her former self. She lay on the floor and hugged her legs against her chest.

Pieces of her life had been torn away from her starting with the death of her parents. She'd lost mentors, lovers, her dragon and now her dignity alongside her eye. All of it bubbled to the surface and she expelled the grief in a fit of tears that wracked her body and stung her charred face. Soon the guards would come to collect her. Until then, Rayna wept until she fell unconscious.

22
Still of the Night

T he evening's festivities became more of a spectacle than Falkon expected. He loved every minute of it. When his father sat the throne, Saltwood Stronghold remained empty save for the staff wandering the halls. Guests weren't permitted inside unless they had business matters to discuss. An evening of relaxation and libations was unheard of under King Favian's rule.

Now that Falkon wore the crown he changed the rules. The kitchen provided the feast, local merchants brought their best intoxicants, and the finest stock of sexual partners came from the mercenaries themselves. Soon the castle looked more like ale houses in Theopilous than a house of royalty.

But it mattered not. There was reason to celebrate. The filthy slayer of dragons had been caught and she would soon pay for her crimes. King Falkon would drag her before the people of Sandhal and dole out punishment until Rayna begged for death. The thought of it made him smile as he leaned back in his throne watching the escapades of the unadulterated.

He yearned to join in but thought to wait until he could slip away to his private chambers. Though he offered a pleasant evening for those in attendance they did not need to observe his dalliances. Some things needed to remain private, especially for a royal. His queen did not seem to share his same sense of modesty.

Falkon watched Nadiuska slip in from the side entry that led to the gardens. She wore a dark purpura gown slit down to her navel. The full sculpt of her bosom was on display for any who dared look. Nadiuska enjoyed having all eyes upon her; she reveled in it. But when the misguided hands of a guest grazed too long near her cleavage, King Falkon stepped in.

He stumbled from his throne with a head full of wine and other intoxicants. Pushing through the crowd he caught the hand that lingered on his wife's breasts and yanked it away. Only then did he realize the hand belonged to Coraise.

"Is this your way of asking me to dance?" he said with a smile.

Falkon released his hand and dared to push him back. The act of aggression caught the attention of the

Righteous Wardens and they began to circle around
Falkon. Undaunted, he continued.

"Why are you being so familiar with my wife?"

To this Coraise laughed and waved off his men. "I
applaud you for finally finding your balls, King Falkon."

"Stop being such an asshole and answer the question."

"I was simply admiring her dress," Coraise told him.

"I don't believe you."

Nadiuska heard enough of their bickering. In their time
together Falkon learned she had a unique way of getting
what she wanted. At that particular moment she wanted
a little fun.

"You two can fight each other tomorrow," she said.
"Tonight why not fuck each other instead? In fact, we
should all fuck...together!"

She took them both by the hands and led them away
from the party. Confused, yet eager, Falkon followed her
to the bedroom with Coraise right next to him. Nadiuska
closed the massive doors then slowly stripped off her
clothing.

At first, Falkon didn't approve of his queen baring
herself in front of a low-class mercenary like Coraise. But
when she set her lips upon his, Falkon's interest grew.
He watched Nadiuska push back Coraise's jerkin to
expose his broad chest. As her hands moved over the
mercenary's body, Falkon's arousal increased. He
wanted to be involved.

151

Stepping over to the duo he set his hands upon Nadiuska's soft bottom and squeezed it. Pleased with his touch, she turned from Coraise and kissed Falkon with a passion he'd not experienced from her before. Her tongue danced over his own and explored the roof of his mouth. He pulled her naked body close to his and moved his fingers towards her wetness.

Not to be outdone, Coraise rejoined the fun. He removed his clothes and pressed his sculpted body against Nadiuska's back. His hands cupped her full breasts and teased the nipples. She leaned back into his touch and kissed him with equal fire.

Falkon slid from his robes to expose his own body. He felt a bit self-conscious standing near Coraise's muscular frame. But Nadiuska welcomed his soft belly and fur covered chest into her embrace. Soon limbs and lips mingled with each other at such a frenzied pace Falkon didn't know where Nadiuska ended and Coraise began.

The first time his hand grazed the mercenary, Falkon was taken aback by his hardness. Then, he grew curious enough to explore him more. Caught up in Nadiuska's kiss, Coraise simply groaned in pleasure from Falkon's touch.

Delighted with the play, Nadiuska moved Coraise's lips from hers onto Falkon's own. The three of them moved to the comfort of the bed where they enjoyed each other in heightened pleasure.

They tasted, touched, and fucked until the large chamber doors pushed open. Intoxicated with wine and lust, Falkon still held enough wits about him to seek the intruders. Coraise as well sat up looking for a fight. Nadiuska simply leaned back among the pillows and laughed.

"You recall my daughters, Xara and Xiamara?" she said. "I summoned them to join us."

The Daughters of Chaos stood in the doorway like a vision from another world. Each was the stark contrast of the other. Where Xara's complexion was fair, Xiamara's was darker. But their appetites matched their mother's.

"We brought extra treats," Xara said with a giggle.

There was a time Falkon held a strong love for her. She captured his heart like no other could. Now, as the girls brought in the remaining two members of the Righteous Wardens, all Falkon could think of was unbridled pleasure with all of them. It was as if his thoughts were singularly focused on the enjoyment of all things. Deeply caught up in his ravenous appetite for food and fucking, Falkon didn't even notice when Nadiuska and Coraise slipped away.

~

The queen took Coraise to one of the guest chambers where they continued fornicating like beasts. Replete and resting naked upon the soft furs his mind began to clear. Whatever fog overtook him in the midst of the party now gave way to a sudden concern for his well-being.

He tried to rush from the bed only to have his cause for concern validated. Nadiuska stood in his path draped in a long, dark cloak of indigo and black gemstones. She gave him a sinister smile and pushed him back onto the bed.

"It's been a long night," he said. "Even I need time to recover my energy before I can perform again."

Nadiuska shook her head and gave a soft laugh as though his statement amused her. Then she revealed a massive broadsword from a sheath at her back. Only one look at the sword and Coraise recognized it as the magical blade that once belonged to the dragonslayer.

At first Coraise thought Nadiuska meant to kill him with it. Then he dared to believe she enjoyed his skills in bed so much that the sword was a gift. A closer look at the hilt revealed the gruesome secret Coraise sensed all along but hoped wasn't true.

He was in the presence of a witch. Now he found himself in her bed and thus her clutches. No wonder he mingled flesh so willingly with those he despised. She cast a spell upon the lot of them to lose their inhibitions and do her bidding.

As much as Coraise enjoyed fucking the queen he

didn't like being used as a puppet. He wanted to leave but it appeared as though Queen Nadiuska wasn't quite done with him yet. Coraise thought about trying to overpower her. He would yank the sword free of her grasp and use it against her. But the more he looked at the sword the less he wanted to touch it.

"The jewel in the hilt," he said, pointing with a shaky finger. "That looks similar to Rayna's dragoneye."

"Not similar. The very same," she told him.

The admission brought wicked glee to her voice. For Coraise, it made him wretch. His vomit was a mix of shame, fear, and intoxicants leaving his system. He managed to tilt his head away from the bedding but almost spewed on the queen's shoes.

"Is there a problem?" she asked, the lilt in her voice replaced with aggravation.

Coraise wiped his mouth and looked up. "Did you rip her to pieces?"

The queen laughed. "Don't be silly. I merely took her eye."

"Why?"

Immediately he regretted the question as she came towards him. He tried to shift over on the bed but she caught his shoulder and kept him still. Then she lifted the sword towards him.

The ease in which she held aloft such a large broadsword wasn't natural. She twisted it so Coraise could have a better view of the eye in the hilt. Its colors waned under the morning sun now entering the room.

"Much of Blahkbyrn's power stems from the dragoneye. Rayna, the fool girl, never quite tapped its true capabilities. Now that the eye is back where it belongs the blade is nearly indestructible and capable of slicing through even the hardest of materials with ease."

Nadiuska decided a demonstration was in order. She made Coraise hold out his own blade and proceeded to cut it in half with what she dubbed Blahkbyrn.

The strength of the blow stung Coraise's hands and caused him to drop his ruined sword to the floor. Off instinct, he quickly covered his bared manhood. This made Nadiuska laugh but she allowed him to dress while she continued explaining the sword's abilities.

"You've seen the fire come to the blade, that's an easy trick. But it's capable of so much more."

"Such as?" Coraise asked, intrigued with why the queen might be divulging such secrets to him.

"Such as melting through solid rock or shooting blasts of fire from the the tip," she continued. "But having the dragoneye embedded in the hilt makes it even more powerful. It contains an energy that is sentient in nature with a consciousness all of its own." She turned to Coraise and smiled with pride. "I gave it that. Using the last of my arcane magic, I fashioned the dragoneye and set it within my champion. Alas, she turned out to be my greatest failure."

Finally, Coraise found the nerve to question her. "Why tell me all this?"

"Because, you fool, you're going to use Blahkbyrn to track the dragon. You'll be my new champion!"

Coraise still didn't understand. "How is that possible? The dragon could be anywhere."

"The same way I kept track of Rayna for all these years," she explained. "With the psychic ability from the dragoneye embedded in Blahkbyrn it is now all-seeing. The wielder of the sword can see anywhere on Atharia. With this ability you can find the baby dragon and resolve this problem that would be otherwise impossible to fix."

Coraise reached out for the massive blade. "Then you're giving me this sword?"

"It only seems fair since I broke yours in half."

When Nadiuska handed Coraise the sword it almost felt as though a transference of power took place. The sword contained much more power within it than the last time Coraise held it. The energy almost flowed from the hilt into his fingertips and throughout his entire body.

Whatever trepidation he felt about the queen before fell away. She regarded Coraise with the worth and respect he rightly deserved. For that, she had his unyielding service. He knelt before her and bowed his head.

"I shall not fail you."

"You needn't do that," she told him. "Rise."

He stood and she kissed him. Then she slapped him across the face drawing the smallest speck of blood from his lip.

"I don't indulge in weak men. In you I sense a hunger yearning to be set free upon the world in glorious chaos."

The queen wiped the blood from his lip with her finger and then licked it clean. Coraise felt a tingling in his skin where she'd touched him. It pulsed through him like a raging inferno until he felt the compelling urge to seek and destroy.

23
Pit of Despair

Rayna heard someone calling her name. The voice sounded a thousand miles away but she could tell they spoke with urgency. Her warrior's instinct caused her to react without thinking. She reached for her sword only to find that it didn't sit at her waist. The confusion brought her out of the fog that clouded her mind.

As she woke the voice grew clearer. Jagger cradled her body against his. He kissed her forehead and pleaded for her to stay with him.

"Where am I going?" Rayna muttered, still unsure of her surroundings.

"Thank the gods, you live!"

He pulled her closer to him and she lay in his embrace as the feeling returned to her body. The ache crept in with slow, deliberate intent. Then it blossomed into an overwhelming churning sensation. Spreading from her orbital socket the hurt pulsed down the side of her neck, deep into the meat of her shoulder, and extending across her torso.

She came to recognize the pain in her chest as more emotional than physical. A part of her had been stolen, ripped away and never to return. For years Rayna hated the bejeweled eye staring back at her in the mirror. She called it a curse, a stigmata. All of that rang true but the dragoneye was also a part of her ethos and thus her being.

It had been with her since her early days like her massive broadsword and her penchant for hunting dragons. Now, like Bhrytbyrn and her duty to dragon slaying, the eye was no more. With its removal, Rayna felt the last bit of herself slip away. The only reason she did not fall into the darkness forever was Jagger.

He kept her awake and alive with stories of their time spent in the Forsaken Force. They were light-hearted youths back then compared to what they became. Jagger focused on the positive tales filled with fun and laughter. It made Rayna long for those days again. Jagger grieved his youth as well. His words grew remorseful.

"If only I hadn't cast you out that day perhaps we wouldn't be here now."

"No sense dwelling in the past."

She spoke more to herself than Jagger but the words

rang true for both of them. They were each survivors in
their own right. Neither could be kept down long
enough for one to claim victory over them. So long as
Ryu remained on Atharia it was Rayna's duty to protect
him. That vow she made to the mother dragon Saarath is
what drove her now.

With Jagger's help she sat up and managed to keep
down some water. It came in a dirty bowl and tasted like
sewage but Rayna didn't care. Any liquid upon her dry
tongue was a welcome relief.

As she drank, Jagger pushed back her dirty blonde
locks and kissed her forehead. She managed to smile at
him then a thought crossed her mind.

"How are you in my cell?"

To that he laughed. "You know no chains can hold me
long. I only let them think they kept me immobile."

"Why not escape?"

"Because getting free of the chains is one thing," he
explained. "Escaping from this wretched place is much
more difficult. I tried early on in my capture. They beat
me severely enough that during my recovery time I
realized I needed to come up with a plan."

"Did you?"

"Yes, but then all hell broke loose. King Favian died
and his son, the odious Falkon Fourpsire took the throne.
Then the witches came and well...."

He brushed his fingertips across her brow and lingered

upon the burned flesh where her eye once sat. Rayna turned away and kept her gaze averted while he talked.

"If I knew that's what he was going to do I never would've let them take you."

"They would've killed you."

"I've escaped death this far," he said. "I must be pretty valuable to them alive."

"More likely that Falkon forgot you were down here."

She didn't mean it to sound harsh, just matter-of-fact. The only reason Jagger didn't have his head sitting on a pike is because Rayna caused King Falkon such grief. Now that he had the former dragonslayer rotting in his cells too, it was only a matter of time before they both died.

While they spoke Rayna gathered what little cloth she could spare and fashioned a new eye patch. They stripped her of her furs and dragon-scaled armor leaving only bits of leather to cover her breasts and below. From that she ripped away what she need leaving only enough to keep her modesty intact.

Only when she had the patch in place did she turn back around. When Jagger saw it he frowned and tried to take it off. Rayna pushed his hand back and scooted as far away from him as her chains allowed. Undaunted, he shifted closer though he stopped trying to remove the patch.

"Why do you cover it?"

Rayna couldn't help but chuckle. "This coming from the man who once called me a demon-eyed cyclops?"

"I was a foolish boy then." He took her hand in his as he spoke and she let him. "I didn't know what I had at the time and I said harsh things I wish could be taken back."

"You were grieving your father."

"Still, when I started to hear about your exploits across this land, and even into Kartha, I knew what a fool I'd been."

"The two of us together could've been unstoppable."

"We still can be."

Rayna did not expect his lips upon her own. Even more so than that she didn't expect she would welcome his kiss. The taste of him took her back so many years before to their first kiss.

Stepping off the training field into Jagger's tent they explored each other with the shaking hands of unskilled lovers. Now they were both well-traveled warriors. They knew that life was fleeting and moments of passion needed to be pursued whenever they presented themselves.

Rayna indulged in her want but only for the moment. Then she pulled away from Jagger. She spoke low so the guards wouldn't pick up anything.

"We need to get out of this place."

"I know but how?"

"You said you had a plan?"

"Yes, the rough beginnings of one."

"Walk me through it. The two of us together can make escaping a reality."

Jagger was concerned. "Are you sure you carry enough strength after everything Falkon did to you?"

"Falkon is the least of our worries," Rayna told him. "His queen ripped out my eye, stole my sword, and is now after my dragon. That is why I cannot sit here another moment. I'm getting out of here if I have to cut my damn arms free of these chains to do it."

"That won't be necessary."

Jagger gave her another quick kiss and then started work on setting her free. While he worked they discussed the plan of escape. Rayna did not intend to let the witch Nadiuska get away with all the pain she caused. But for now, her vengeance would have to wait. First, she needed to find Ryu.

24
Dark Desires

The evening's festivities left King Falkon light-headed and slightly ashamed though eager for more. He sat upon his throne listening to the page drone on about the problems the people of Sandhal were having. None of it mattered.

Once his head cleared he would bring out the dragonslayer for their amusement. He would be heralded a true king, loyal to his word, and rightful monarch. Falkon knew some still spoke ill of his family heritage. Many wanted to see him ousted from Saltwood Stronghold and thrown back into the sea from which he came. Having the dragonslayer as his prisoner would silence the naysayers.

As his page concluded recalling the list of grievances, Falkon adjourned to seek his wife. Queen Nadiuska had been wandering off quite a bit as of late. Falkon paid it no heed until she slipped away with Coraise Kennethgorian. Having the mercenary around indefinitely was out of the question. Let him collect his pay and leave Sandhal.

But in that remedy existed a problem. Falkon didn't have the pay he promised the Forsaken Force. Truth be told, he never expected them to fulfill their part in the agreement. Rayna was too skilled to be captured by a rag-tag group of mercenaries. Somehow Coraise proved him wrong.

When Falkon found Nadiuska he meant to explain the situation to her. But she was in such a jovial mood that Falkon didn't want to bring her down. It was rare to find the queen with a smile on her face and a song in her voice.

She stood out on the open deck adjoined to their quarters looking over the land. Falkon poured them each a goblet of wine and joined her. They toasted, and drank, then stood quietly.

"The people are restless," Falkon said, breaking the silence.

"Their needs don't matter to me now that I'm so close to getting everything I desire."

Her answer seemed strange. Then she softened and smiled. Turning to kiss his cheek she altered her response to tell him what he wanted to hear.

"But if you feel it necessary then indulge them their

whims."

"I want to show off the slayer," he told her. "To show them what this house is truly capable of."

Her eyes sparkled like twin gemstones under the midday sun as she stared at him. Then she stroked his beard and glanced another kiss off his cheek before giving a strange response.

"Do as you please. I'm done with her."

"What does that mean?" he asked.

Nadiuska ignored the question and began to leave. Falkon set aside his wine and went after her. He caught her by the arm and repeated the question, this time with authority.

"What does that mean?"

She pulled her arm free and glared at him until his bones chilled. The longer she stared, the more Falkon felt as though he were back out on the Graven Peaks under the falling snow of an avalanche. He hunched over and hugged himself trying to warm his body.

"You don't seem yourself, my love," Nadiuska said. "I hope you're not growing ill in the same manner your father did."

"Of course not," he replied, surprised to hear his teeth chattering as he spoke. "He died of an old man's ailment. I am a young man still. It's just the previous night's indulging catching up to me is all."

"Pleasure begets pain."

On that cryptic note, Nadiuska left their chambers. She didn't answer his question nor even bother to help him with his illness. Falkon had enough of his wife's constant disrespect. He knew if he wanted to command authority under his rule it would need to start with his queen.

25
No Return

Jagger made good on his word helping Rayna free of her chains. The next bit proved tricky as they needed to slip past the guards and into the halls. Fortunately, a celebration of sorts was being prepared and the guards were called away to assist. This left Rayna and Jagger unattended.

"You would think they would keep better watch on their prize possession," Jagger joked.

Rayna didn't find the humor. Something seemed off as though they were being led to slaughter like lemmings. Still they pressed on moving silently through the lower chambers of the castle.

It took Jagger many long days moving only inches at a time to map the underbelly of the castle. But he committed to memory every area where they might be seen by the staff. Kennels would need to be avoided along with the kitchens.

Around the next bend sat the sleeping quarters for most of the staff. They slept almost ten to a room with beds stacked atop each other. It was here that Jagger brought them.

"Are you mad?" Rayna said in a harsh whisper. "They are liable to be going in and out. We'll be seen."

"We're just going to borrow some clothes so we can go upstairs without arousing suspicion."

His plan made sense. It was obvious Jagger spent a long while coming up with the smallest of details so he could escape clean. They began rummaging through the clothing bags of the staff looking for uniforms to wear. Jagger found a stable boy's garb while Rayna was left with a servant girl's dress.

As they began to change she hesitated. A grim realization fell upon her and she couldn't bring herself to continue. Jagger sensed her distress.

"What's wrong?"

"My eye...or lack thereof," she explained. "I'll be spotted immediately."

"Trust me, you're not the only one-eyed person held up in this castle," Jagger told her. "The punishments run deep and dark under King Falkon."

"It's not the king who concerns me."

He set a reassuring hand on her shoulder. "I know. But the way we're going the witch won't be anywhere near us."

With fresh clothes to mask their appearance the two started towards the stairs. They moved past the kitchen with haste though the cooks were so busy with preparations they wouldn't have noticed anyway.

Taking each step two at a time they reached the top without any problem. It was too easy. Surely someone noticed they were missing from the cell. Jagger didn't share Rayna's concern. He was so certain of his plan that he couldn't see any warning signs.

"Once we head through the door we'll have to run towards the map room," he said. "Inside sits a hidden tunnel that will take us directly outside the city."

"I knew this castle held secret passages."

"You did? Why didn't you say so?"

"I've only seen the main route through the large fireplace in the throne room," she said. "I didn't think you would want to go there."

"Probably not but still a good bit of knowledge to have."

Jagger turned the handle and swung open the door only to find two ethereal looking women standing in their way. One held dark features while the other was fair-skinned. They dressed in opposites and wore their hair in contrast as well. But it was their magic which concerned Rayna the most.

With the flip of her hand the dark-haired beauty sent Jagger tumbling back down the stone steps. Then it was Raya's turn. The blonde one took her by the throat and lifted her up. She looked Rayna over, almost sniffing her, before tossing her down the stairs as well.

Each step found a soft spot or a sensitive bone to strike. Rayna did her best to cover her head but even that got rattled. Jagger caught her as she fell down the last remaining steps into him. Both of them looked back up at the ones who blocked their way.

The women appeared to glide down the stairs rather than walk. They caught up with Rayna and Jagger within seconds. Then the punishment continued. Jagger took nails across the cheek while Rayna felt a sudden knee strike. Their pain provided the women with enjoyment.

"You two rats didn't think you were escaping did you?" the blonde one asked.

"It took a great deal of effort to find you, dragonslayer," the other said, yanking off Rayna's eyepatch. "We're not letting you leave before your party."

"Come now, you're both the honored guests and the entertainment."

With that they took both Rayna and Jagger by the scruff of their necks and led them like children. Though they looked diminutive, the strength that resided within them could not be matched by human hand. Now Rayna knew who held them. These were the Daughters of Chaos.

26
A Pirate's Price

For the first time since his father claimed Saltwood Stronghold the gates were open to the public. Shop owners, farmers, and citizens of Sandhal all converged on the castle to witness the unveiling of the dragonslayer.

King Falkon and Queen Nadiuska stood at the top of the steps looking down over the crowd. The guards at each post were doubled and archers placed upon the towers. No one would make a move on the king and queen without being stopped dead in their tracks.

Pageantry was slight with jugglers and joke tellers moving swiftly. Falkon wanted to get to the main course of the day in a hurry. He could already hear the adulation from the crowd in anticipation. But before Rayna was brought out the Righteous Wardens made an appearance.

Coraise and his men pushed through the crowd headed

towards the king and queen. As they advanced, Falkon grew tense. He noted a larger number of men in Coraise's brigade than before. A few rough looking women also joined his cause.

The look shared between Coraise and Queen Nadiuska also unnerved him. They kept a secret between them that Falkon wasn't privy to. That would be the first thing that ended when he laid down his new rules. For the time being, he welcomed Coraise and the Wardens as his esteemed guests. Then he greeted the crowd.

"I know you've all been waiting in anticipation of what's to come. Let us not dally any longer. Bring out the dragonslayer!"

It gave Falkon great pleasure to hear of Rayna's attempts to escape. That meant the fire in her belly once again roared. Snuffing out that fire in front of a capacity crowd would bring him great satisfaction.

But when the Daughters of Chaos led Rayna, and her companion into the square, Falkon reeled in surprised. Where the jewel-like dragoneye once sat only a scar remained. The flesh was charred around a gaping wound that drew sympathy from the crowd.

"What is the meaning of this?" Falkon asked turning immediately to Nadiuska.

"Rayna carried something that I needed," she explained. "Now finish this display. I have important matters to attend."

"No wife. This is unacceptable!" Falkon shouted. "I promised these peasants the legendary slayer, not some wounded warrior who gains their favor."

"What difference does it make? You're going to kill her anyway."

"I can't kill her. I need to use her as payment for the mercenaries."

Though he tried to speak under his breath, Coraise still caught his words. He was none too pleased with what he heard.

"What madness do you speak? You expect to give me the girl as payment after everything promised?"

"Coraise, hear me out. She'll fetch you quite a profit on the slave stocks. You'll have more gold and jewels than you ever dreamed of."

"What good is a one-eyed slave?" Coraise argued. "Even I don't find her appealing anymore."

Falkon searched his mind for an answer that could appease all. Truth be told, he just wanted the mercenaries off his back. He would deal with Nadiuska later. The people had seen the slayer. They knew their king kept his promises. Better to get the disfigured woman out of their sight swiftly. Then an idea came to him from his days as a seafarer.

"There is a man who will pay you handsomely for such a slave," Falkon explained. "His name is D'zdario Dizdar."

"The pirate? They say he's a scoundrel. How do you know he'll pay?" Coraise asked.

Noting Coraise's growing interest Falkon spoke fast. "My father gave Dizdar his first ship. He owes my family. Besides that he has alot of gold and always finds slaves useful no matter what they look like. I'll even throw in the other one and you can name your price. Dizdar will pay, I promise you."

Coraise thought it over. As he ruminated Nadiuska continued to argue.

"I want the girl dead!"

Finally, Coraise came to terms and defied the queen in the process.

"No, I did as you asked. I shall be rewarded for it."

He shook hands with Falkon then took his leave to fetch a gift that would calm the queen. Falkon didn't know what gift he spoke of but so long as it got Nadiuska off his back he didn't care. Now he needed to persuade the people that Rayna would be punished for her crimes.

27
Dragon Heart

F alkon argued with Coraise and the witch. It would've been the perfect time to break free and try for an escape. But the Daughters of Chaos stood too close. Without her blade Rayna could do little against them.

Too much magic had overtaken the city. She felt traces of it the first time setting foot inside Saltwood Stronghold. Rayna didn't know it then but King Favian was under a dark spell. Now that Nadiuska infiltrated the castle even stronger magic permeated the air. It gave Rayna chills upon her flesh.

Then she heard them speak of the pirate D'zdario Dizdar. That caused her to shake even more. The way the dreaded pirate tortured his slaves was legendary across the land. If they were to be sent to his ship they would never make it back alive.

Jagger noticed her discomfort and nuzzled his head against her. That small movement gained him a strike across the brow. Rayna cast her eyes on the bitch who hit him. The blonde one, who she'd come to know as Xara, blew her a kiss in response. Not wanting to miss out on the fun the other one, Xiamara, pushed Rayna's face.

"Eyes forward," she said.

The odds were overwhelming. Even the crowd was against them. People shouted and spit at Rayna. Spoiled fruit, rotted meat, and even human wasted was flung at her. Rayna remembered how revered she was the first time heading through the gates of Sandhal. The people loved her then. Now they wished for death and dismemberment. All of their vitriol built by lies from the king.

With an apparent deal made between King Falkon and Coraise, the king spoke to the crowd. He chastised Rayna for countless crimes that she did not commit. The most heinous charge of all lay in the killing of Valerios the Valiant whom the people adored.

If they knew the truth about Valerios' death they would storm the gates and tear down the false king. Instead, they threw more shit at Rayna. She took it all without showing any weakness. Jagger got pelted just for being an acquaintance of Rayna's. He cringed and almost gagged from the smell.

"Don't give them the satisfaction," Rayna whispered.

"It's horrid," he replied. "Why don't they just kill us already?"

"They have something worse in mind. We're being sold to D'zdario Dizdar."

Jagger dropped his head into his chest. "We're fucked."

Falkon told the people of his intent to have the mighty dragonslayer sent away to sea. He detailed the ways in which Dizdar would break both her body and her spirit. It wasn't enough to satisfy the blood thirsty crowd. So he decided to give them what they wanted.

At Falkon's request a beating commenced on Rayna and Jagger. He had his guards use fists and feet to strike them both bloody. Then wooden batons were brought in to increase the pain. The crowd erupted in cheers as wood struck flesh causing purple bruising and swelling. Rayna did her best to cover up but the blows kept finding sensitive spots. Finally, mercifully, the call was made to stop the beating.

"Enough of this!" Coraise shouted. "I can't sell dead slaves."

King Falkon waved off the guards and then stood with hands raised in some sort of victory. He basked in the cheers from the people as he stood over Rayna's battered body.

"Get them ready for transport and then bring them to Coraise." He squatted down to look Rayna in the face then whispered: "I got you, bitch!"

They didn't bother offering any care to the prisoners. The blood dried and the throbbing ache in Rayna's head subsided on its own. Large metal shackles bound her wrists while a length of chain ran from them up to another shackle upon her neck. Jagger was also chained in similar fashion.

They couldn't fully extend their arms without it pulling on their necks. The awkward position increased the pain of Rayna's injuries. If they were to get out of this mess she wondered if she would ever heal up right.

Scraps of food were provided so the prisoners didn't starve to death in transit. They forced them to eat like dogs hunched over and chewing from bowls on the floor. Rayna marked every humiliating moment intent on returning the favor double to each and every one of them. As they ate Rayna whispered an apology to Jagger.

"I'm sorry I got you in this mess."

"What do you mean? I was in that cell long before you came along."

"Yes, but you could still be down there plotting your escape," she said. "Now they have you lumped in with me, an extreme threat to the throne."

"I would rather be with you." He gave her wink then said: "Besides, we're not done yet. There is always a way out. I just have to find it."

No sooner did they finish their meal that they were

brought before the king. The guards forced them into the
throne room and onto their knees. King Falkon rose from
his chair and walked the length of the hall to greet them.
He moved slowly to savor the moment having Rayna on
her knees before him. Once he stood before them he
frowned in disgust.

"Get something to cover that gruesome eye," he
ordered. "We don't want Dizdar to think we're slighting
him."

"Now why would he think that?" Coraise asked
walking into the room. "If you're sending me into a trap
I swear by the Source Gods I'll send my ghost back to
haunt you for all your days."

"Relax, Coraise. Everything is savvy, I swear it,"
Falkon told him. "Word has been sent to Dizdar and he
is routing his ships here as we speak."

"He was just waiting in the port then? What if I didn't
agree with your offer?"

"I didn't set you up. Dizdar doesn't waste time with
long sailing trips. He prefers to be near the coast
awaiting passing ships they can sack."

"I dunno why anyone would want to live at sea
anyway." Coraise looked over to Rayna. "Send me a note
and let me know how you like it, luv. Alright?"

"Fuck you."

He shook his head. "I'm no longer interested in doing
that with you. However, I do fancy your companion."

Jagger shriveled at the inference. Coraise corrected his assumption. The alternative was so much worse than Rayna expected. K'lani was brought in by the Righteous Wardens. She struggled as they dragged her across the floor.

Rayna tried to reach out to her only to have the chains bite into her neck. She called the girl's name and K'lani looked her way. Terror was etched upon her face. Her eyes no longer held the innocent sparkle to them. Something happened to her out in Atharia and Rayna felt guilty for it.

"Where is Ryu?" she cried out, praying that the little dragon was safe somewhere.

K'lani shook her head and Rayna felt herself weaken at the thought of his death. The nobles and mercenaries stood round them laughing at their despair. Rayna straightened up as best she could. She wouldn't give them the satisfaction of breaking her. But then Nadiuska arrived.

Dressed in robes of dark eminence she glided across the floor towards the gathering. Behind her came the Daughters of Chaos. Each of them held the sides of a large steel cage and inside sat Ryu.

Rayna screamed in defiance and tried to charge them. She was met with a baton to the thigh causing her to fall on her face. Upon seeing her Ryu began crying out. Undeterred, Rayna started crawling towards him. She made it all the way to Nadiuska's feet where the queen kicked her hard under the chin.

Her teeth gnashed together and sparks of darkness filled her head. She came in and out of consciousness. Bits and pieces of conversations echoed throughout the throne room. Both K'lani and Jagger were calling for Rayna to wake up. Ryu shouted and shook the cage to no avail. The royals had them all.

28
Dread Pirate

R ayna's entire body tensed and agonized with a desperate need to be reunited with Ryu. It took four guards, one at each limb, to drag her from the throne room. She fought against their grasp until one of them struck her in the mouth. Her head fell limp and all she could do was shout for her dragon through fits of tears.

"Silence, or I'll strike you again!" the guard warned.

Rayna refused to fall silent causing the guard to pick up his hand. This time he slipped on a metal gauntlet intent on shattering her teeth with a backhand. Surprisingly, Coraise Kennethgorian stopped him.

"No," he said wagging a finger at the guard. "Even D'zdario Dizdar won't accept a toothless woman. Just wrap a gag around her mouth."

The guard seemed agitated that his need to strike out

went unfulfilled. Still, he did as Coraise asked of him. It left Rayna with a wrap covering her eye and her mouth. Closed in on herself with only grief to keep her company she wept.

The royals won. They broke her down to the marrow and left her with nothing. Her sword, her eye, her dignity, and now her dragon were taken away by the filthy hands of King Falkon and his queen bitch. Rayna the Dragonslayer was no more. Noting her distress Jagger tried to rally her.

"Don't give up, Rayna. I'll get us out of this."

"Quiet or we'll gag you as well."

The warning silenced Jagger's mouth but Rayna knew his mind remained at work. Still, she no longer held the will to carry on. Better to die out on the sea than live a life of servitude at the hands of the most ruthless pirate that ever lived.

They were brought down to the docks where Dizdar's ship, The Widowmaker, sat anchored a few feet from shore. His was an Admiralty ship gifted by King Favian the First. It was modified for cannon power, Rayna counted twenty-four in all.

Additional changes were made to enhance speed and ensure faster boarding capabilities.They had strengthened the hull, put up three masts for larger sails, and removed various partitions to improve stability.

Around seventy to ninety men were on board. Each

one fulfilled a specific need on the vessel and they were rewarded for it. Rayna, Jagger, and K'lani's reward for hard work would be to keep their lives.

D'zdario Dizdar waited for them on the dock alone. The sheer size of this man told Rayna he didn't need anyone to back him up. Dizdar stood at least a foot taller than Coraise Kennethgorian, himself a tall man.

Dizdar wore his long, dark hair pushed back in multiple braids. A thick beard peppered with gray hung from his chin. Sleek leather arm cuffs wrapped his forearms. A patchwork of furs and soft leathers were stitched together for his shirt and trousers. It looked as though he wore bits and baubles from every treasure he'd looted in his days of pirating.

The weapon of choice hanging from his belt is what caught Rayna's attention. A whip of around twenty inches long sat comfortably wrapped up on his hip. It had an oak handle braided with beef skins. The whip itself was a macabre display of bone fragments weaved together to resemble a human spine.

As the group of them made their way down the deck, Coraise began telling his Wardens to stay sharp. From his tone it was clear he didn't trust the merits of the deal King Falkon brokered for them with the rogue pirate.

Dizdar laughed at their approach. A deep, guttural laugh pulled from his belly and caused him to double over. His reaction caused confusion and the Righteous

Wardens halted.

"This is what you've brought me?" Dizdar asked, still unable to stifle his amusement. "I expected three mighty warriors and instead all I see are drown rats."

Coraise waved his Wardens back and motioned for the Saltwood Soldiers to bring the prisoners closer. Dizdar folded his burly arms across his chest and waited on them. Rayna kept her gaze trained on the crudely fashioned whip hanging from Dizdar's belt. If she could get her hands on it that provide them opportunity to fight back.

But Dizdar kept his distance. No doubt he wanted to have a wide enough berth to draw weapons in case of attack from the other side. Coraise did the same coming only close enough to unleash his sword if needed. Only now did Rayna realize the sword he carried used to be hers.

The greatsword, saddled with the odious name of Blahkbyrn and set with the dragoneye in its hilt, rested at Coraise's back. Rayna's arms tingled with the need to hold her sword. The sensation increased and she knew it could only be quelled when the blade was in her hands again.

When the chance to reunite with Bhrytbyrn came she would be ready. For now the guards carried Rayna and her companions like livestock to the slaughter. From the way that Dizdar looked them over he felt about the same.

"These are some of the finest stock you'll ever run across in the slave trade," Coraise reassured him. "I present you Rayna the mighty dragonslayer."

They tossed Rayna at Dizdar's feet. He looked down upon her with steel gray eyes. She met his stare with her one good eye but could not hold his gaze. Full of weakness, shame, and despair, her head dropped from her shoulders as she awaited her fate. Dizdar chuffed in disappointment.

"What else you got?" he asked Coraise.

Stammering as he tried to close his sale Coraise hyped up his other pieces of merchandise. First they pushed Jagger forwards with the unearned title of 'king of thieves' attached to him. Dizdar did not show interest. He pulled on his beard and remained silent as he motioned for the last in line to be presented.

Growing notably aggravated, Coraise pushed K'lani forwards himself. She stiffened her body and tried to keep her head down. Rayna heard the girl muttering prayers. She feared for K'lani as Coraise built her up with tales of exotic lands from which concubines learned their trade. This caught Dizdar's attention.

"Very nice."

"We have a deal then?" Coraise sounded relieved.

"Yes, we have a deal."

As the two clasped hands to make it official Rayna felt her heart sink. She always thought her days would end in a blaze of dragon's fire. Never did she expect to be sold like a breeding mare to be ridden and worked until death.

29
Of Wind and Water

Dizdar instructed a small rowboat be dispatched from his ship. It came across with a few of his lieutenants and officers. Sacks of gold coins also made the journey. There at the docks the trade was made official. Coraise got his pay and the prisoners were transported by rowboat to The Widowmaker.

They weren't permitted to speak while in the boat though Jagger kept breaking the rule to check on Rayna. A strike across his cheek and the threat of being thrown overboard is what got him to stop. Dizdar paid no attention to them. He spoke at length with his lieutenants in hushed, clipped words Rayna couldn't decipher. Pirates often created their own language so others wouldn't be privy to their conversations.

When they reached The Widowmaker, the captain boarded first. Then one-by-one the prisoners were hauled up by their arms and tossed onto the deck. Rayna's body had grown numb to the abuse. But as her shoulder hit the wooden planks the pain reinstated itself.

The wound had not been properly treated since the Kappa sunk its teeth into her flesh. Scarring from the bite puckered her flesh in the interim but as she tumbled across the deck it tore free. She winced as the heat of fresh pain radiated through it. One of the lieutenants, a burly man with sheer cropped hair, noticed her reaction and took special interest.

"They sold you damaged goods, sir."

Captain Dizdar patted the man on the shoulder then pulled Rayna to her feet. He marched her around in a circle for all the crew to cast their eyes upon. She felt more exposed by this display than if she were stark naked.

"Don't you know who this is?" he asked, presenting her like a cut of beef. "This is Rayna, the mighty slayer of dragons. She's bested all the winged beasts across Atharia and proudly wears the scars from those encounters."

Dizdar ripped the cloth covering from Rayna's mouth. Then he pulled her so close to him she felt the coarseness of his whiskers against her cheek. The smell of tobacco laced through his words as he spoke in a dark whisper upon her ear.

"Or are those tales just a heaping pile of horseshit you

created to fetch a profit?"

When Rayna didn't answer he pushed her back down to the ground and stood over her triumphantly. The crew laughed at her misfortune and cheered on their captain in his mock victory.

"Now the dragonslayer is mine!"

Again his lieutenant questioned his purchase. "She smells like rot."

"Have her swab the head. She can clean up the shit stains," Dizdar told him. Then he turned to Rayna: "You can be the slayer of shit!"

The crew of The Widowmaker erupted in laughter again at Rayna's expense. She did not care. The humiliation was nothing compared to the ache of loss spreading through her like a fungus. Ryu's crying still rang on her ears. Now that the witch held him, hope was lost.

As the ship began to disembark, Dizdar continued handing out jobs for their new prisoners. He deemed Jagger able-bodied and good for hard work. The crew made certain he knew the beatings that awaited him should orders not be followed.

Then D'zdario Dizdar turned his attention to K'lani. She shivered in fear and tried to keep her gaze averted but he would not have it. Grasping her chin in his massive hand Dizdar looked her over with a lustful gleam in his eye.

"This one is the real prize. Those fools didn't even realize what they had," he said. "A true princess of Ischon. Emperor Kivu Kazu will pay handsomely for her return."

Dizdar pushed back K'lani's dark hair with his fingers to see her face clearer. Then he ran his tongue up over her cheek slowly to savor the salty taste of her. Her disgust of his actions pleased him to the point of arousal.

"Or maybe I'll just keep her for myself."

Taking K'lani by the hair Dizdar dragged her across the ship. The crewmen kept Jagger and Rayna restrained forcing them to watch as their companion was taken below decks towards Dizdar's cabin.

With their entertainment concluded the crew went back to work. Rayna marched along as they pushed her towards the head to clean up waste. The men chuckled and some dropped their trousers to add to the mess for her.

Over the laughter and the crashing waves Rayna heard K'lani crying out from below. Something in her screams struck Rayna's ear in such a way that it roused her from the haze of defeat. She couldn't stand the thought of the girl being violated while she stood by and did nothing.

The minute the seafarers handed Rayna mop and bucket to begin her duties she reacted. She learned long ago that anything could be used as a weapon. The mop became her sword and the bucket a makeshift flail. She started on the fools with their pants down.

Quick strikes to the back of the head or knees caught them well enough to keep them out of the fight. At least two fell overboard and were swallowed by the sea. Rayna continued her attack with long swings of the mop to disarm the men as they drew their weapons.

One of the short swords skidded up to Rayna's feet and she capitalized on it. Tossing the bucket of suds into the face of the first mate, she snatched up the sword and started hacking. Across the ship Jagger began his own dance of destruction. He used speed and ingenuity to avoid being overwhelmed by the crew. They tumbled into each other and fell over the railings as Jagger moved swiftly between them.

The shit stained deck now ran red with blood. Rayna forced her way through the pack and down towards the cabins. Dizdar's lieutenants blocked the way. These were formidable opponents who didn't earn their titles by chance. Rayna knew their skills would be far superior to the rabble she just cut down.

Fortunately, she had help. Jagger swung in from off the main sail and kicked one of the lieutenants in the face. He took a tumble down the stairs to the lower decks. The remaining man, the burly lieutenant, stood in Rayna's path.

"I knew you were going to be trouble," he growled.

"You have no idea."

Off instinct, Rayna pushed back her eye patch to try and ignite her sword. With no eye and the wrong sword in hand it didn't catch fire. But the charred flesh over her missing eye distracted the lieutenant long enough for Rayna to strike. She slashed him across the throat creating a thin smile of blood on his neck. He dropped his sword which Jagger collected before he and Rayna hurried down below deck.

The other guard regained consciousness just in time to get stabbed through the face. From there Rayna hurried towards K'lani's screams while Jagger turned around to hold off the rest of the crew. The sounds being made from the captain's cabin were guttural and raw like an animal. Rayna braced herself for the horrible scene she was about to walk in on. When she kicked in the door she found an unexpected surprise.

K'lani stood over D'zdario Dizdar with a dagger in hand. He lay sprawled across his bed with several stab wounds across his bare chest. K'lani's clothing was torn and covered in the man's blood. She drew ragged breaths through her nostrils like a jungle cat.

Rayna approached her slowly so as not to frighten the girl. She touched K'lani's shoulder feeling the still warm blood that stained her skin. The girl jumped back and held the tip of the blade towards Rayna in defense.

"It's me," Rayna told her. "Lower the knife. You're safe."

K'lani's wild eyes tried to register what Rayna was saying. She started to lower the knife when Jagger ran into the room. He slammed the door behind him and started to barricade it.

"We're not safe," he said, refuting Rayna's claim. "There are too many of them."

Her mind searched for a logical answer but found only violence. She reached down and snatched the bone whip from Dizdar's belt. The weapon felt foreign in her hands with a fluidity to it that would take some getting used to. Rayna preferred the heft of her sword but being backed in a corner she would make due with the macabre whip.

"We'll have to fight," she said. "There's no other way."

"Let's jump," K'lani told them.

While Rayna was pleased that the girl no longer seemed catatonic her suggestion didn't make sense.

"Jump where? Into the ocean?"

K'lani nodded with a renewed confidence Rayna hadn't seen in her before. She began prying the deadlight from the scuttle. Seeing this, Jagger tried to talk her down.

"We'll drown out there, K'lani," he said. "Besides, the scuttle is too small to fit through."

She paused in her actions. Jagger's words made sense and K'lani knew it. But she didn't abandon her plan altogether. She grabbed the prone body of D'zdario Dizdar and dragged him towards the scuttle.

"What're you doing now?" Rayna asked.

"The wood is rotted here," K'lani explained. "If we throw the captain's body at the wall it should produce a sizeable hole for us to climb through."

"And take our chances in the sea?"

"Rayna, you have to trust me on this."

K'lani spoke with a calmness and certainty that Rayna couldn't ignore. The pounding against the door grew louder. It was only a matter of time before the crew broke in and tore the three of them down. It seemed they had little choice but to follow K'lani's lead.

"Jagger, help us with the captain." Rayna said.

"We're seriously going through with this?" he asked.

"There are no other options. The numbers are too great and I do not have the power to fight them all off."

She hated to admit it. There was a time in her life when she fought as one against an army and succeeded. To run from a fight didn't sit well with her pride. But Rayna also knew how to read the signs of battle before engaging. This helped her stay alive when stalking dragons across Atharia.

Jagger hurried over and helped them lift the mass that was Captain Dizdar. With calculated movements they threw him with all the strength they carried into the rotted wood planks. Just as K'lani expected the wood buckled from the impact of his weight. A man-sized hole remained and Dizdar himself disappeared into the water below.

"I pray the Goddess of Water lets us live to fight another day," Jagger said.

"It is the God of Wind to whom you should pray," K'lani told him.

On her words, K'lani linked hands with her companions. Then she began speaking in a language unfamiliar to Rayna but one she'd heard before. As she spoke, a strong pull of air enveloped the three of them. Before Rayna could understand what was happening a gust of wind pulled them from the ship.

30
Tears of the Dragon

N adiuska thought having Rayna bound in chains and groveling before her was a treat. But finally getting her hands on the red dragon filled her with even more bliss. The room just off the royal chambers is where her plaything was chained up. She kept him inside the castle away from prying eyes but close enough to fill her needs.

For now, she only wanted to look at him and revel in her capture. Once he was chained up inside the room his squawking finally stopped as though he suspected what was happening. That wouldn't keep Nadiuska from having her fun.

She paced in front of the dragon watching its green eyes track her with such a want of destruction. Bound safely out of reach he could only sit in compliance while she derived pleasure from his pain.

"You've grown swiftly," she told him. "It's been difficult to tell with Rayna blocking my view from you. But now you're all mine."

At the mention of Rayna's name the dragon shifted against his chains. He sniffed the air and tried to seek out his pseudo-mother. Nadiuska sat back upon a cushioned chair and poured a drink while she watched the realization of loss fall upon him.

"She's gone. You're never going to see her again. Just like your birth mother." Nadiuska paused and sniffed her drink then smiled at Ryu. "Oh wait, that's not entirely true. Part of your mother is here now."

She tipped the crystal chalice towards him to showcase what rested inside. A magical elixir Nadiuska waited years to imbibe again. The dragon crooked his head in confusion so she spelled it out for him.

"This is the last bit of your mother's blood. I had her brought here to me where I could savor every last drop."

With that the queen drained her drink. The dragon's blood invigorated every cell of her body. She felt a renewed jolt of power tingling throughout her fingertips ready to lash out upon the world.

While she drank Ryu began to shout and struggle against his bonds. Insulted by his interruption she threw the empty chalice at him and then dared to approach.

"You're next!" she warned, point her finger towards him.

With astonishing speed, Ryu snapped his jaws and almost bit off the tip. Nadiuska drew back just before he caught her. She staggered back bumping into the chair and knocking it to the floor.

A sneer crossed her full lips but she didn't lash out. She needed to save the dragon until he grew large enough to sacrifice. During that time she would take a taste every now and then to keep her power from fading. But she couldn't just slaughter him outright. He was the only remaining dragon on Atharia and she would make him last.

As she turned to exit the room a different problem presented itself. King Falkon stood in the doorway looking over the scene with disgust. He stepped inside and closed the door behind him eager to confront Nadiuska with all the angst that had been building between them.

"What goes on here?" he asked, his voice lifted into forced authority. "I thought you had slunk off with Coraise again but now I see this. You're holding a dragon inside the castle without my consent?"

"He's my pet. I do not need your consent."

"It's a dragon, Nadiuska," Falkon argued. "Both my father and my best friend perished because of a dragon hunt and you bring one inside our home? I cannot allow this."

Nadiuska heard enough. It was clear that Falkon felt a

rift forming between them. He was losing control of his queen and his kingdom. In a last effort to take back his power Falkon thought to force his rule. Except he held no power over Nadiuska and never did.

She grew tired of pretending to be the doting wife. Now that she had the dragon, and Rayna was shipped off to sea, the games could cease. It was time for a new rule to commence.

"Foolish king," she said backing him up against the door. "Your father and friend were killed by your own hand. Not because of dragons and not because of the dragonslayer. They died because of your petty jealousy and lust for power."

Falkon was taken aback. "Lies."

"Search your thoughts, you know it's true."

She grazed his brow with her fingertips and let him see the truth. Her daughters had buried his actions deep in his mind making it easier to guide him like a puppet. Now he saw what he had done to Valerios up on the Graven Peaks.

Falkon's own sword is what killed his friend. Angered by Valerios' friendship with Rayna, it drove Falkon to do his worst. The blade plunged deep into Valerios' belly while he stood unarmed and defenseless.

The king tried to pull away from Nadiuska but she increased her touch. Setting both hands upon his head she forced him to see more. The death of his father came at his hands as well. He drove a massive dragon's tooth into King Favian and killed him in his own throne.

Nadiuska forced him to see the double murders multiple times until Falkon could feel the physical extension of both. He cried out causing the dragon to begin screaming as well. Not wanting to draw anymore attention to the forbidden room, Nadiuska silenced King Falkon for good.

She let him feel the pain of impalement that he wrought on his victims. The pressure of it built until his organs failed under the strain. It was as though Falkon stabbed himself though no blade had been drawn.

Eyes wide and blood dripping from his mouth, Falkon made an attempt on Nadiuska's life. His hands wrapped around her throat with the intent to strangle her. But it was too late. The king succumb to his internal injuries and dropped to his knees.

Nadiuska pushed him aside. "Long live the queen."

Things moved faster than anticipated. It became time to enact the final stages of her plan. She summoned her Daughters of Chaos to the room. They arrived on wisps of air and settled next to the body of King Falkon.

At first, Xara appeared shaken by his death. Apparently she had grown to care for the king while embracing her mission of controlling him. When she saw her mother's disapproval, Xara let her feelings fall away.

"It's time, girls," Nadiuska told them. "As you can see

King Falkon is no more. We have to hurry to enact our spell upon the castle before his body is found."

Her daughters nodded and the three of them linked hands. They began an incantation summoning arcane energy from a dark void no human would dare cross into. Behind them the dragon flapped its wings in a desperate attempt to fly free. But the chains wrapped around his neck and legs kept him still.

The witches continued chanting with fervor pulling more energy the faster they spoke. Soon the skies outside turned gray as though storm clouds rolled over the city of Sandhal. The concentration of energy shifted over Saltwood Stronghold. With fresh dragon's blood in her veins it allowed Nadiuska to extend the spell. Soon Cragstone Keep where the soldiers slept was enveloped as well.

After a few minutes more the spell was set and the entire castle staff enslaved, including the guards. Nadiuska and her daughters hugged each other in celebration. Too long had it been since they were able to conjure such fearsome magic. Now the power of their once great coven returned to them. It was their time to rule.

"Come my daughters," Nadiuska told them. "Gather the dragon and let us leave this place."

With all of Sandhal under their spell they set out in covered wagons with a caravan following close behind them. The Saltwood Soldiers brought up the rear as they marched towards the Majestic Mountains. Finally, Nadiuska and her daughters would return home.

31
The God You Know

Being pulled so abruptly from the broken hull of the ship startled Rayna. She expected to feel the coldness of the ocean slap her in the face as they fell within it. But they never reached the water. Instead, and to a much bigger shock, the three of them hovered on air.

"Hold onto me and don't let go," K'lani said.

It became clear that she was the one keeping them from falling into the ocean. What Rayna didn't understand is how she was doing it. Then they began to move on air in jagged spurts.

Rayna did not like heights. She cared even less for being out of control of her movement. Clutching onto

K'lani for dear life is all she could do. Jagger as well felt out of sorts as they flew across the air.

The combined weight of her companions didn't slow K'lani down. She found her rhythm and glided like a bird towards safety. Soon they found their way to the water's edge. There the three of them tumbled to the shore.

Rayna scrambled from the water grateful to be on land. Jagger crawled up next to her and lay against the sand. He laughed with relief in such a way that Rayna couldn't help but join him. They lay there cackling like crazed fools until K'lani approached. Her shadow cast down over the two of them like an ominous apparition.

"We have to move," she said dusting sand from her bare legs. "I didn't bring us far enough away. The pirates will turn the ship around and they will find us."

Rayna sat up and stared. The girl was a mystery from across the sea on Ischon though she no longer looked like an innocent traveler. Her dark hair pulled loose from from the tight braid at her back and fell wild across her shoulders. A slit in her trousers exposed bruised knees and her tunic remained stained with Captain Dizdar's blood. As disheveled as she looked there remained an urgency about her that could not be denied. Still, Rayna had questions that needed answers.

"How did you do that?"

"What does it matter?" Jagger said, jumping up from

the sand. "We're free!"

Rayna stood and dusted the sand from her rear. "It matters to me."

K'lani gnawed on her bottom lip once again showing her youthful innocence. This time Rayna would not be swayed. She believed all along the girl from Ischon was hiding something. Now she would find out exactly what.

"Are you a witch?"

The bluntness of Rayna's question made K'lani gasp. But the tactic worked and she wound up speaking her truth.

"I come from the land of flying warriors in Ischon," she explained. "There we have a great connection to the God of Wind. He blesses us with these special traits."

"You can fly. Don't you think that's something you should've told me before?"

"It's not flying, more like gliding, and I can only do it in spurts on Atharia."

"Why?"

"Because the Source Gods have all but vanished here." K'lani frowned. "I can barely feel the presence of the God of Wind. There is a much darker, more vile energy encompassing this land."

Rayna shuddered. Her fingers traced the water-stained patch upon her face remembering the disfigurement beneath it and who was responsible.

"It's witchcraft you feel," she said.

"Yes, but I am no witch."

"I believe you."

Jagger interrupted them. "Ladies, let's move this along. K'lani was right about the pirates."

He pointed out across the sea where The Widowmaker could be seen in the distance. The bow of the ship pointed towards shore. Either someone on deck spotted them or made a guess on the whereabouts of their escaped prisoners. Regardless, they were headed towards them and fast.

Gathering the limited weapons they had the trio rushed from the area. Rayna was both relieved and disgusted to find the whip of bones still in her possession. With K'lani in front of her as they ran she could see the long scars upon her back and legs. Captain Dizdar got a few strikes in with the whip before meeting his fate.

It unnerved Rayna to carry such a vile weapon. But she needed to have something for defense. Still, she longed for the familiar heft of her sword, the reassuring feel of the hilt against her palm. She hurried to catch up to K'lani eager to ask more questions. It was a bit of a switch from their first encounter.

"Where did you get the dagger that killed the captain?" she wondered.

"It's yours. The one you keep at the small of your back," K'lani told her. "I took it from you the day we met in Valeuki. You must not use it often if you didn't realize it was gone."

Rayna snatched the dagger from K'lani's hands and looked it over. Sure enough it held the same jagged grooves and leather wrapped handle as her own.

"This is indeed my dragon dagger," Rayna admitted. "You have very skilled hands, K'lani."

"I'm pleased you think so."

Rayna smiled then flipped the dagger around and handed it back to K'lani. She hesitated to accept it until Rayna insisted.

"Go on, it's yours now," she said. "Just don't tell me where you've been hiding it this whole time."

K'lani hugged the knife to her chest as though she received a piece of gold from a treasury. Rayna marveled at her two companions as they walked on in front of her. They looked like drown rats but each stood by her on this forced quest. It gave her a renewed sense of spirit and belonging.

That level of care for another is something she hadn't experienced in a long while until Ryu came into her life. When she lost him to the witch Nadiuska it felt like a mistake to open her heart again. But when she was ready to give up both Jagger and K'lani wouldn't let her. Rayna felt a kinship with them; a bond that couldn't be easily broken. So she knew when called upon they would have her back once more.

"We need to return to the castle."

They paused in their trek to turn and face her. They looked exhausted and beaten but remained ready to fight.

"The witch has taken Ryu," Rayna continued. "I must get him back."

"You made a pact to keep him from harm," Jagger said recalling the tale Rayna told before in the cell. "I make that same vow to you now."

"I as well," K'lani told her. "But Rayna, what happens if the witch has already brought harm to Ryu?"

She didn't want to think of such things but she already knew the answer to the question.

"Then the pact is revenge!"

32
All the King's Men

I t took them the remainder of the night to return to Sandhal. By then the pubs would usually be raucous with the townspeople enjoying themselves. But when they arrived at Sandhal Square it remained quiet. No lively tunes were played; no jovial fun was had.

"This is peculiar," Jagger whispered as they strolled through the empty square.

"There's a chance the queen knows we've escaped the ship," Rayna told them.

"How?"

As uncomfortable a tale it was to tell, Rayna let them know all about her dragoneye and what Nadiuska did. Before they began to pity her with comforting words she continued to speak of the eye's power.

"It can see far across Atharia," Rayna explained. "Right

now the eye could be trained on us, watching as we approach the castle."

"If that was true wouldn't the guards be swarming upon us?" K'lani asked.

Off instinct the three of them checked over their shoulders and into dark alleys as they passed. No patrols lurked in the streets. They appeared safe for the time being.

"Perhaps the queen lied to you."

Rayna shook her head. "No, I've felt the power of the dragoneye. I remember its pull. Even years before I felt guided in some way. That's why I began wearing the patch. I needed it to stay docile lest I go mad."

"I thought you covered it because some fools reacted to it like disgusting pigs with harsh remarks."

Rayna knew that of which Jagger spoke. When he first saw her without the patch many years before he referred to her as a demon-eyed cyclops. His words stung and he cast her out of the group she considered her family. From then on Rayna relied only on herself. But she was starting to see the value in having companions to rely on. So, she wanted Jagger to know she no longer felt bitter about his actions.

"That was many years ago and we were just children," she told him.

"Still, I am sorry for how I reacted."

She set her hand on his shoulders and looked him

square in the eyes. The grime-ridden patch remained firmly in place over a part of herself she would never reveal again. But that was all in the past and they needed to move forward.

"I forgive you," she told him. "There is no need to dwell on it further."

To Rayna's surprise Jagger reached out and hugged her. She hesitated to return his embrace then found herself melting into it. Then K'lani jumped in for a group hug. The three of them remained there in silence to revel in the moment before heading towards Saltwood Stronghold. Once inside the castle they would be facing their biggest challenge yet. It stood to reason that not all of them would be making it out alive.

~

On Jagger's lead they made their way to an unmarked path just outside the castle gates. It routed around the side towards the stables. This is where they would make their way into the castle rather than trying to storm the gates.

"Those secret passages I was telling you about let out here," Jagger explained. "All we need to do is slip in and we'll find our way near the cells."

"So long as we aren't back inside them," Rayna replied.

"Agreed."

The entry to the secret passage was found under a false

panel by one of the horse stalls. As Jagger worked to find it Rayna and K'lani kept the horses calm. The last thing they needed was to have one cry out and alert the stable hand. Or worse still an agitated horse could rear back and kick Jagger in the head.

"It's here," Jagger told them from the back of the stall.

As he moved the floorboards aside Rayna flashed back to the Kappa dragging her underground. It caused her to balk when Jagger and K'lani started down inside.

She struggled with following them. Only then standing alone in the quiet of the night did she realize the castle grounds were barren. No soldiers patrolled the area or even stood at the gates. Something felt very peculiar but Rayna couldn't settle on what it meant.

Jagger and K'lani motioned for her to follow them into the passage. After a few deep breaths to calm her nerves Rayna climbed inside. She replaced the false panelling behind her and the three of them edged forward. Narrow tunnels kept them crouched low and scurrying like rodents.

After a few sharp turns and one misstep they arrived at the other end. Slowly, Jagger pushed aside an iron grate and stepped out into the room. After checking the area for guards he waved the others through. K'lani went first with Rayna behind her. When she stepped out she found herself within the throne room and not near the cells as expected.

"I must've misunderstood the layout," Jagger said almost apologetically.

"It doesn't matter," Rayna told him. "At least we're inside."

They replaced the iron grate and then inspected the empty throne room. It felt cold and ominous as though only spirits walked the halls.

"What's happened here?" K'lani asked, rubbing her shoulders to keep the cold out.

"I will tell you," a shaky voice said.

At first when the voice called out they couldn't discern whether it were real or imagined. Then it grew louder punctuated by a coughing fit that sounded like a death rattle. As they followed the sounds they found it coming from upon the dais.

King Falkon Fourspire sat slumped in his throne. His crown lay at his feet and blood stained the front of his silk shirt. The coloring of his skin looked gray making him appear fresh from the grave. So when K'lani and Jagger drew their respective weapons, Rayna surprised herself by showing him mercy. She told them to stand down while she approached the throne alone.

"Rayna," Falkon almost choked on her name. "I should've known you would escape. Even the dreaded Captain D'zdario Dizdar was no match for the dragonslayer."

"Actually, K'lani killed him," Rayna said, causing the

girl to beam with pride. "What happened here, Falkon? You look as your father did the day I met him: with one foot in the grave."

"It seems my father and I weren't so different after all," he explained. "I betrayed my father; my queen betrayed me."

"Nadiuska did this? I'm not surprised."

He tried to nod and almost fell over in his throne. Rayna had to push him by the shoulder to force him back up. K'lani and Jagger moved closer expecting a trap but Rayna could tell the king would soon be no more. But she was going to get answers before he perished.

"Where is the queen?"

"Left, bewitched my kings guard and took them with her."

Now it made sense why the town and the castle were so quiet. Nadiuska swayed everyone to her side whether by barter or spell. Now she had an army of her own marching off towards the unknown.

"My dragon?" Rayna asked hopefully.

Falkon reached out a shaky hand and grasped Rayna's arm. She felt the weakness in his touch. It almost made her pity the man to see what he'd become. But if anyone deserved such a fate it was the king who killed his father, and his best friend, to ascend the throne.

"I'm sorry, Rayna," he said. "Had I known what Nadiuska, or her daughters, were really after I never would've...."

Rayna pulled her arm away. "Yes, you would've. A coward, drunk with power, does many things he only feels shame for later."

"This is true, but I've tried to make amends."

From his robes he pulled out a parchment. Once unrolled it revealed the bounty decree placed upon Rayna's head. The words were altered by ink to declare a pardon on her. In her place, queen Nadiuska was now the one being sought after.

"My last act as ruler is to lift the bounty from your head and place it on that bitch, Nadiuska," Falkon said. "Kill her and you can have all the riches you've ever desired."

"I don't care about riches," Rayna told him. "I just want my dragon. Where did she take him?"

Rayna leaned in towards his face until she could smell the death coming off him. She did not care. Had the fool just left her in the tavern so many moons back she would not be in this predicament, nor would he. Now there was no turning back.

"Where is Ryu?" she asked again, gripping the lapels of his royal robes.

"Rayna, enough," Jagger said. "Let us leave this place."

"I'm not leaving until I know where she's taken Ryu."

Jagger touched her arm compelling her to step away.

"He's no use to us. If the queen left with an army we

can track her ourselves."

"Not if she used magic to shield her movements."

"I may know a way around that," K'lani told them. "But I agree with Jagger, we should go now."

Rayna knew they were right. Once again she trusted in her friends to keep her on the correct path. She glared back at Falkon Fourspire one last time. He tried to avert his gaze but she caught him by the chin and forced him to face her.

"May you see your father again."

His eyes widened in fear and then teared up. More blood dribbled down from his mouth as his head bowed low. King Falkon would be dead soon.

"I was surprised to hear you leave him with such pleasantries," Jagger said as they left the throne room.

"I didn't," she corrected. "He hates his father. May the two of them battle each other for eternity in whatever fate awaits such scum."

Knowing that the guards were gone, and the staff scattered into the wind, they ransacked the castle. Facing a witch and her army would take much more than they carried from Dizdar's ship. But even if by some stroke of luck they found a full satchel of weapons they would still be inferior.

Rifling through the quarters of the Saltwood Soldiers they found everything mostly picked clean. Then off a subsection of the tower a private room was located. It took Jagger a few moments to pick the lock but when he got it open they found a plethora of treats.

The room was setup in a tidy, structured manner with a back wall full of books. While K'lani and Jagger gathered what they could Rayna took in her surroundings with a heavy heart.

"This room belonged to Valerios."

At her words K'lani stopped and said a silent prayer for the fallen. Jagger also ceased his actions though he didn't understand why the mood shifted.

"Who's Valerios?"

"Someone I once knew," Rayna explained, her eye welling with tears. "He was a good man. Gone now. I didn't see his quarters the last time I was here. It feels strange as though he's still here."

"He's not," K'lani said bluntly. "So he won't mind if we take what we need."

Rayna shook off the emotions weighing on her. K'lani spoke true; Valerios wasn't there. It was foolish to place the breadth of a man's life on material things. He was so much more than that.

Fortunately for them it seemed King Falkon kept Valerios' room off limits after he died. That left them a treasure trove of items to ready themselves. Jagger found a sleeve shield that ran over his right shoulder. He replaced his worn-out boots with a pair of Valerios' lined with fur and reinforced with armor plating. A handheld axe and a leather pleated skirt rounded out his gear.

K'lani found a pair of leather pants that fit her well enough when belted. A lightweight coat with custom pauldron armoring also suited her frame. Once again she tied back her dark hair as she began fixing Rayna's dragon dagger to the end of a blunt staff.

"Turn it into a spear. A wise idea," Rayna told her.

Now it was Rayna's turn to gather arms. She knew Valerios would keep his finest garb tucked away for safe keeping. In his mind, he was going to travel back across the sea to Ischon where his betrothed Kemi awaited him. That meant trunks would be packed and ready for travel.

On the first one opened she scored a bounty of clothes for the taking. Though it felt strange to wear a dead man's wardrobe she proceeded anyway. The warrior woman dressed herself in ornate black and gold armor over simple leathers covering her hips and breasts. She wore tall boots extending over her knees. A cape of skins dyed red sat at her back to guard her from a sneak attack.

To finish the job, Rayna refreshed her battle appearance. She tied back her hair in fierce braids and used ash from Valerios' smoking pipe to apply war paint upon her face. Her gaze remained stern, her jaw set tight as she readied herself to face the witch and her minions.

Armed, and full of supplies, the trio set out in search of the witch before she blanketed Atharia with her horde of murderous puppets. As they left the castle Rayna took one last glance back at the throne room. There King Falkon sat slumped in his chair, dead.

She grunted in approval. Let him rot until nothing remained but a skeleton dressed in tattered threads. With the king out of her way now she could focus on bringing an end to the witch who'd been tormenting her since birth. One way or another the dragon curse would be ended.

33
Quest of Dragons

Rayna hoped to find the witch Nadiuska immediately after they left Saltwood Stronghold. Jagger did everything he could to make that happen. They had taken the horses left behind at the castle and rode hard to catch up. But Atharia is a big place and the witch had a sizeable lead on them.

It took days of tracking before he stumbled upon anything worthwhile. The lead wasn't much but at least he could return to Rayna this time with a sliver of hope. He hated to see her feeling defeated. After everything that happened to her with the witch taking her eye, losing her sword and her dragon, Jagger wanted to be able to make everything good again. He owed her that much.

After three days of searching the farmlands for any

clues they took refuge at an old farmhouse. According to Rayna it was run by a kind man named Josep. He let her take shelter there before when she was on the run from King Falkon's bounty hunters.

Now word spread across the lands that the bounty was lifted. Though no one seemed to care one way or another. From what Jagger heard the kingdom was in disarray with Falkon's untimely death. It was only a matter of time before it all came crashing down.

When they reached the farm Rayna was saddened to find Josep had died. The only consolation came with it being a natural death. She would've never forgiven herself if soldiers murdered him while searching for her.

But Josep had been gone awhile. That meant his crops had failed and the farm itself was in disarray. Still, it gave them a place to rest away from the elements. Rayna made it a point to give Josep a proper burial at the back of his property. She thanked him for helping her before and his hospitality now. Then she set Josep to eternal rest.

K'lani scrounged the pantry for food and was able to cobble together some tasty meals. Between the two of them they tried to keep Rayna's mind off Ryu and what the witch might be doing to him. For all their efforts she remained singularly focused.

As Jagger rounded the path up to the house he found Rayna sitting out on the stoop. Every night since they squatted there she would sit outside and smoke the vile sythian weed. Of all the things they found in Valerios the Valiant's room the ashwa was the worst of it.

Rayna offered her pipe to Jagger and he waved it away. The stench alone made him want to be sick. Besides, his father always told him to remain clear-headed. Indulging in ashwa or too much ale dulled the senses and Jagger wanted to keep his mind as sharp as his blade.

"I'm surprised to see you smoking so much of that," he said sitting next to her even as the smoke stung his lungs.

"It calms me."

Her reply was even, emotionless. He worried that she would shut off and go into her dark shell. Not wanting to waste anymore time he told her what he found on his trek.

"There are multiple tracks heading up towards the sea where Watersnake River lets out."

"They took a ship?"

"No. They separated. The larger party continued west while a smaller band on horseback went east."

"Then we should track the larger party. That's where the queen will be and Ryu with her."

Now the delicate part. "I don't think it's wise to go right after the main caravan. We should hit the smaller patrol first and gather any information we can that will help us infiltrate the queen's forces."

To Jagger's surprise Rayna agreed without an

argument. Perhaps the ashwa leaf did some good after all. They decided to settle for one more night at the farm to get some good rest before chasing down the patrol.

During the night Jagger began to worry that Rayna only placated him with words to mask her true intent. He knew her well enough to be concerned that she might slip out and go after the queen herself. His thoughts troubled him so much he couldn't rest. Finally, he got up to see for himself if Rayna had disappeared during the night.

There were two bedrooms in the home. They could've easily doubled up so everyone got a bed. But Jagger let the girls have the rooms and he took an old armchair downstairs. He wanted to keep eyes on the entry points in case of raiders. Ever since his father was killed in an ambush on their home, Jagger didn't sleep well.

Now he had another reason to keep him awake. Rayna had just come back into his life. He wasn't about to let her out of it so soon. Creeping up the stairs without a sound he moved to the main room off the landing. Slowly he pushed open the door and peaked in.

To his relief the bed was full. Rayna slept soundly. Or did she? He wouldn't put it past her to arrange a pile of rags beneath the blankets to throw him off. Stepping further into the room to check he tripped on a loose board and stumbled. He caught his balance but the boards groaned beneath his weight.

"You might as well come all the way in, Jagger."

Rayna sat up and stared at him. She left her armor resting on a nearby chair with only her leathers modestly covering her body. The drape of the blankets hugged her curves with just the hint of her bosom showing. Her blonde hair was free of the war braids and fell loose across her shoulders. From his vantage point, Jagger could see the shine of the moon cascading across her face in a magical illumination. He longed to be with her but he knew now was not the time.

"Sorry, I didn't mean to wake you," he said. "I was just checking."

"Thought I might slip out in the night to fight my battles alone?"

"Something like that."

"That's not who I am anymore." She paused then patted the bed beside her. "Join me."

As much as he wanted to Jagger steeled himself against the invitation.

"I shouldn't."

"You should," Rayna argued. "We all need a good amount of rest before tomorrow. Sleeping in that beat up old chair isn't doing you any good."

"I'm fine, really."

"Don't argue with me, Jagger."

Finally he lamented. Closing the door behind he slipped into the bed beside Rayna. They both lay back against the stuffed pillows, eyes staring at the ceiling. Rayna shifted her weight until her back was to him. He turned to the opposite side and stared at the wall. It would be even more difficult to get proper night's sleep with Rayna's warm body next to him.

"Jagger," she said, her voice a whisper on the air. "Hold me until I fall asleep."

Turning back over he did as she asked. Pressing his body against her own he marveled at the taught musculature she'd developed. Rayna was just a girl when he knew her before. She struggled to understand the world and even herself. Now she was a battle hardened warrior. Still, as he wrapped his arms over her, he could sense the gentleness residing within her. She held him tight and before Jagger knew it he had fallen asleep.

~

When morning came Rayna did not speak of what happened with Jagger. It was a momentary lapse in judgement from smoking so much ashwa. She wanted his familiar touch to remind her of a time when things looked promising. Her selfish need may have been misinterpreted for something more. For that she regretted her impulsive behavior.

Jagger didn't mention what happened either. For that, he earned Rayna's respect. She could tell he wanted to speak with her about it but knew more pressing matters faced them.

Once they were packed and ready the three of them left the farmhouse behind as they sought the witch's patrol party. Jagger took point following the tracks he discovered the day before. The search led them up towards the shoreline where neither boats nor man traveled much.

As they drew closer Rayna caught sight of movement. A group of soldiers meandered around the edge of Watersnake River. Seeing them as well Jagger slowed his horse. Rayna and K'lani caught up with him and the three assessed the situation.

Rayna counted five of them all dressed in dark leather and armor. Multiple blades and axes sat upon their backs or rested at their hips. They were an armed militia ready to do battle. Rayna was certain this group followed Nadiuska's orders.

"What're they doing?" K'lani asked.

"Pissing in the river," Jagger told her.

"That's gross!"

"Maybe," Rayna said. "But it's the perfect opportunity to get a jump on them."

They slipped from their horses and tied them off on a nearby tree. Then, using the thick marsh as cover, the trip edged towards the unsuspecting soldiers. But as they drew closer Rayna halted her companions.

"Those are not Saltwood Soldiers," she told them. "It's the Righteous Wardens. That means Coraise Kennethgorian is nearby watching."

Sure as she mentioned him, Coraise made an appearance. He trotted up from further north on a mare of pure white. Rayna watched him as he spoke to his Wardens. Something in his mannerisms looked off. His eyes were glassy and he swayed back and forth as though uncertain in the saddle.

This was not the leader of the Righteous Wardens that Rayna encountered so many times before. His men also had the faraway look in their eyes. K'lani noted their strange appearance too and it troubled her.

"They're under a spell."

"We can use that to our advantage," Jagger said. "If they're being puppeted by the witch they won't have their usual fighting style."

K'lani disagreed. "No, they will be even more powerful. There are spells which can enhance a fighter by diluting his fear response. It makes them aggressive and unstoppable."

Rayna thought back to all the times she sought dragons to slay. In those times she felt fearless and ready to die for her cause. She wondered if the witch set the same type of spell upon her in order to carry out her bidding.

"No one is unstoppable," she said. "This is our best lead to find Ryu and I'm not letting them slip away."

The others agreed. Without a second thought they charged from the marsh and attacked the Righteous Wardens without remorse. Coraise followed his usual battle strategy to turn tail and run. This led Rayna to believe he wasn't under a spell afterall. The witch would not let him depart if she were controlling Coraise.

Rayna went after him using one of the Wardens' horses. They galloped out of the marsh, across the sand, and right up against Watersnake River. Any closer to the edge and they would've fallen in.

Coraise seemed to be goading Rayna to come after him. He would fall back and then force speed to keep her guessing. The taunting only proved to anger her. She pressed her horse harder than the animal was used to causing it to buck.

Even with the choppy ride Rayna held fast to her steed and increased her approach. Coraise glanced over his shoulder as she grew closer. The look in his eyes appeared hazy, not the bright shade of green she was used to.

Seeing this made Rayna snap. If the queen were inside Coraise watching as she'd done with Rayna for so many years then she wanted the bitch to know she was coming. Standing in her saddle Rayna took a chance and dove across to tackle Coraise from his horse.

They plummeted into Watersnake River and were immediately dragged downstream. This didn't stop

Rayna from attacking Coraise. She hit him several times in the nose with a closed fist. It threw his head back under the water. He came up thrashing about and for a second Rayna saw his true self return.

Grabbing Coraise by his long hair Rayna dragged them both towards the shore. He tried to fight against her grip but the rushing water became his enemy. It flooded into his mouth and eyes causing him to panic. Rayna's strong arms and legs pushed through the current to the embankment with Coraise in tow. She forced him up first before following close behind.

Once they were both on their feet the fight continued. Coraise took a wild swing and Rayna retaliated with a strike to his chin. He staggered back from the blow then turned to his weapons.

When he unsheathed his sword Rayna was disappointed that he no longer held Bhrytbyrn. Still, having a blade in hand made Coraise much deadlier. Rayna went for the only weapon she carried to even the odds. Pulling the bone whip from her belt she snapped it towards him as a warning. He didn't listen and charged towards her.

In that moment Rayna realized K'lani had been right about the spell's power. She knew Coraise as a cagey fighter. He took his time in battle waiting for the perfect opening. This shell of his former self rushed in with reckless abandon.

Rayna sidestepped his advance and wrapped the whip high around his throat. Bracing her legs in the dirt she held on tight as though taming a wild horse. Coraise dropped his sword to engage the whip with both hands.

Stepping further back Rayna pulled on the whip which brought Coraise to the ground. He squirmed and clawed at his throat as the airway constricted further. Having dispatched their enemies, K'lani and Jagger found their way to the scene. At once they called out for Rayna to stop. Jagger even went so far as to shake her.

"Stop it, you'll kill him."

Rayna glared at Jagger in disgust. "He deserves it."

"We need him for questioning," Jagger pleaded. "Coraise is the only one who will know where the queen took Ryu."

Ryu's small face played on Rayna's memory. He'd been so helpless when he was first born. She'd taken him on a journey intent on protecting him. During that time he grew in size but also upon her heart. All she cared about now was getting him back. If that meant Coraise would live another day then so be it.

She relinquished her hold on the whip and allowed him to breath. The sudden rush of air returning to him made him vomit in the grass. When he finished expelling his innards Coraise became docile. K'lani braved approaching him to look deep in his eyes.

"His true self is in there but far away," she said.

"How are we going to get any answers from him then?" Rayna asked.

"We need to break the spell."

"Unless your god can give you the answers to the witch's spell we're lost. I should've just killed him."

"There is another way but it will mean traveling to the magic markets."

"In the Shadowed Highlands?" Jagger questioned. "No one travels up that way on purpose."

"I've done it before," Rayna told him. "But it's far and will take us out of our way."

K'lani shrugged. "It's the only way I know how to break the spell."

"Why can't we just keep tracking the queen to whatever hole she crawled into?"

"Because I never found her tracks," Jagger admitted. "I just wanted you to think I did so you wouldn't lose hope. She must've shielded her movements with magic as you said she would."

"The magic markets will have the answers we need for that as well," K'lani added.

Rayna's frustrations grew. The longer they took to find the witch Nadiuska the more jeopardy Ryu would be in. She hoped that he could sense her energy looking for him. He needed to hang on just a little more.

"Bind Coraise," she said. "We're taking him with us."

They collected their horses and any useful items

scrounged from the fallen Righteous Wardens. Rayna was surprised how much carnage was strewn about the area. It seemed Jagger and K'lani were more than capable of holding their own in a fight.

She was glad to have them riding with her. It would take everything they had to traverse into the Shadowed Highlands and make it out alive.

34
Magic Markets

T reading back into the Shadowed Highlands brought up memories Rayna would've preferred forgetting. At least this time she had people she could trust with her not a pack of ruthless soldiers. Coraise was the exception. If his true wits were about him he would've tried to escape by now.

Instead, he sat stone faced upon the horse as they led him along. If the queen were residing inside him like a dark passenger she had already abandoned him.

One saving grace lay in the fact that they would not be veering towards the Graven Peaks. Rayna didn't have any interest in facing the Shadax again. The last time she ran across the creatures it didn't end well.

K'lani's intricate, almost obsessive, study of maps helped out alot as they traversed further. The magic markets were in a town called Mako, hidden to any but those who knew what to look for. The only way to find them was through spellcasting. This kept those who would otherwise do the magic merchants harm from finding the markets at all.

They passed through a clearing of gnarled brambles only to find their path blocked. Nothing but large walls of stone jutted out in all different directions. K'lani dismounted her horse and walked forwards.

"We're here," she told them.

"It's a dead end," Jagger replied.

Rayna held a hand up to quiet him. "Give her a moment."

In their short time together Rayna came to learn K'lani was highly skilled and intelligent. If she had an instinct, Rayna trusted it as if it were her own.

K'lani knelt down and began whispering on the evening air. Rayna assumed she was making another plea to the God of Wind. She never found much use for the Source Gods. More than once Rayna called for their help only to be disappointed. But as K'lani told it her people held a special relationship with all of the gods.

She proved that to be true now as once again her prayers were answered. Suddenly, as if appearing from nowhere, houses carved deep into the soft volcanic rock appeared. Hundreds of homes sprung up showing an entire community dug into the caves. Rayna was impressed.

"Behold the magic markets of Mako," K'lani told them with a smile.

"I expected something different," Jagger said dismounting.

"They don't have stalls out in the open like most markets," K'lani explained. "Here there is no bartering. You pay the expected price or you go."

"Let's hope they have what we're looking for."

Rayna dismounted as well and the three of them entered Mako. They kept Coraise close and bound by the hands. As they moved further inside the area seemed to grow in size. With all the dwellings residing in the caves it was impossible to know which to approach.

Once again they leaned on K'lani. Her whimsical demeanor was charming in this environment. Each merchant they passed received a smile and an earful from K'lani until they pointed her onwards. Soon Rayna started to feel annoyed as though they were being run around in circles.

"I think it's time I start cracking heads," she whispered.

K'lani waved her off. "You can't come in here trying to slaughter everyone. There's no telling how strong their magic is. Let me handle this. Why don't you two find some food and lodgings for the night."

Jagger and Rayna exchanged looks. How they would find food in such a desolate environment was a guess for them both. But they found their way out of tougher predicaments in the past. Now would be no different regardless of the thick fog of magic on the air.

With Coraise trailing behind them like a brain damaged horse they searched the grounds for some nourishment. No pub or eatery was in sight. In fact, nothing stood out in the open just as K'lani said. Rayna wondered whether K'lani just wanted them to take a walk so they wouldn't interfere with her business.

"Shall we start knocking on doors?" Jagger asked. He was only half kidding.

Rayna shrugged. "We have enough food packed. Let's just find a spot to settle."

"Maybe one of the homes is unoccupied."

"Maybe."

"So, we're back to knocking."

As they walked through the town of Mako, Rayna felt heavy stares on them. The merchants looked from windows and corners observing the strangers. She didn't know whether these people were friend or foe. But instinct told her to trust no one and be ready for a fight.

Tired of walking they found a quiet corner and waited for K'lani to return. They sat Coraise on the ground in front of them while Rayna indulged in some ashwa. Once her pipe was filled she offered Jagger a taste to which he declined.

"I'm staying sharp."

"I've found the herb increases my concentration."

"Or just dulls your wits."

"If that's true then you should abstain. You don't have any wits to spare."

They joked and reminisced about the past for awhile until K'lani found them. She approached with a small man by her side. He wore gray silk robes that flowed with the movement of his body. A matching hood was kept low concealing his face. K'lani stood a foot taller than the man but that meant little in the world of magic. His might be a visage conjured to throw off unsuspecting travelers.

Rayna tamped her pipe and stood. Her hand rested on the whip at her side while Jagger readied his sword. K'lani smiled at the two of them then pointed the small man towards Coraise. He began prodding the catatonic warrior and muttering to himself.

"What is he doing?" Rayna asked.

"This is Elden," K'lani explained. "He says he's willing to help out."

"He can break the spell?"

"Yes."

Rayna turned her attention to Elden. "How?"

He stared up at her and only now did she see his peculiar face. His cheeks and jaw had sharp lines to them as did the bridge of his nose. A thin mustache grew long into a sculpted white beard. His bushy eyebrows twitched as his pale eyes looked Rayna over. Then he turned to K'lani and spoke in a language foreign to Rayna's ear though the girl understood it.

"Ah, he says there is a potion that can be made but he needs a specific ingredient to make it."

"Ask him what he needs and we'll provide it," Rayna told her.

K'lani related the message to Elden. He responded with excitement then began pointing towards Rayna.

"He says it's an herb."

Elden pointed again this time focusing on the clay pipe Rayna held. She pulled back her hand and cringed at the ask.

"Oh, ashwa," K'lani said, familiar with the herb from her homeland. "Elden says he will need the ashwa to make the potion."

"How much?"

"All of it."

Elden smiled at Rayna. His long mustache curved up over his cheeks the wider he grinned. Frustrated, and certain they were being played, she hesitated on handing over her stash.

"If you don't give it to him we'll be stuck here looking for another merchant," Jagger whispered.

They all knew the ashwa wasn't meant for the potion. It was their payment for services rendered. Rayna obliged the strange little man and handed over all the herb she pilfered from Valerios' room. Elden thanked her and scurried off towards what she assumed was his home.

"If I don't get a spell breaker from this exchange I'm going to turn him upside down and shake him until I get my ashwa back."

"I've already warned him of your temper," K'lani told her. "Elden said the potion won't be ready until the morning. He said we're welcome to sleep in any of the empty spaces."

She pointed out which domiciles weren't occupied and the three of them settled down for the night. The sleeping quarters were small, dark, and dank. Rayna wondered if all the merchants in the magic market were little people. Or perhaps they kept their guest rooms uncomfortable so unwanted travelers wouldn't be inclined to stay.

Stripped of her armor with her boots set aside Rayna couldn't sleep. Without her ashwa to calm her nerves she found it difficult to relax in the unfamiliar surroundings.

The bedding was little more than stacked furs upon the floor. The discomfort exasperated the wounds on her back and shoulder. They healed over with dense scar tissue that would leave permanent marks upon her body. Rayna counted them as more badges of honor showcasing her will to survive.

Her eye would never be the same again. Perhaps if Nadiuska hadn't cauterized the surrounding tissue it could've been treated. But between the burns, and trauma involved in her eye's extraction, there was little to be done. Maybe the magic merchants could fix her with a permanent eye patch.

She shifted to her side trying to prop her arm beneath her head for support. No position felt comfortable. Restless, she slipped from her dwelling to visit Jagger in his. She found him having the same trouble sleeping.

"How much do you want to bet that K'lani is sound asleep?" Jagger asked as Rayna crawled up next to him.

"I wouldn't doubt it. She has a unique way about her."

Rayna stretched out with her hands behind her head and feet crossed at the ankle. Jagger mimicked her pose. The two of them stared at the emptiness of the ceiling as they spoke. Keeping their eyes averted from each other helped loosen the tongue to truths.

"I never really expected to escape from King Falkon's prison," he admitted.

"But you seemed so sure of your plan."

"There was never any plan just rumblings from other prisoners. I'd given up hope of ever getting out of there. Only when I saw you did I start trying to figure out a means to escape."

Rayna shifted to her side. "I'm thankful you were there to guide me. I don't know what I would've done without you."

Jagger turned to meet her gaze. His hand fumbled in

the darkness until it rested upon her cheek. The
roughness of his palm felt inviting upon her skin. Rayna
set her own hand upon his then moved it down upon the
slope of her breasts.

"Are you certain?" he whispered.

"Yes."

Jagger shifted closer until his body pressed against hers.
The heat coming from him seeped into Rayna and let her
relax into the moment. His hand wandered across the
fullness of her breasts then explored with more intent.
He lingered at her belly before sliding further down. She
closed her eyes as he teased her causing a shiver as his
fingers darted inside. Rayna shifted up on her elbow and
leaned in to kiss him.

His lips were soft as she remembered from the first
time they kissed years before. But his technique had
remarkably improved. His tongue mingled with hers in
a sensual dance of desire that had Rayna aching for more.

She stripped off her leathers while Jagger removed his.
He lay her back upon the furs and followed with his own
body. With one fluid movement Jagger entered her. He
moved with a delicate grace as Rayna wrapped her legs
around his hips. The discomfort of the bedding became a
distant memory as they found their rhythm.Their bodies
locked together threshing as one with each movement.

Rayna's back arched as she took Jagger in deeper. A
fevered energy built to the insurmountable and then

washed over her entire body. She bit off a scream so as not to call attention from the magic merchants close by.

Jagger buried his head within the length of her hair. She felt his hot breath upon her ear as he grunted in pleasure. Rayna cried out again this time allowing it to escape from her parted lips. Jagger followed close behind her with a shudder that tensed his entire body. They lay replete in one tangled mass of limbs and that is how K'lani found them the next morning.

"Wake up!" she shouted.

Rayna shifted up reaching blind in the dark of the domicile for her weapon. Jagger sat next to her shaking off a heavy drowsiness. K'lani covered her eyes and tossed their gear towards them.

"While you two were busy fornicating the prisoner escaped."

They scrambled to get dressed and followed K'lani outside. The binds that held Coraise had been severed and he was nowhere in sight. Rayna went from overwhelming ecstasy to a deep seeded rage. Whoever helped Coraise escape was going to pay with their life.

35
Dream Dust

Jagger lifted the rope from the stake where Coraise was tied. Obvious cuts were evident meaning someone set him free. He knew whom the blame would fall on. It was easy to attack the one who tied the prisoner but Jagger wasn't going down without a fight. The first stone to be cast was his.

"These ropes have been cut. Small incisions made from a serrated blade. The only one with that type of weapon is you, K'lani."

His accusation caused the girl to erupt. She stalked forward taking wild swings at his face. Rayna had to hold her back before she made contact.

"How dare you accuse me of such things. You're the one who suddenly showed up to sway Rayna to your side...and your bed."

"Bite your tongue." Rayna pushed K'lani back almost knocking her to the ground.

"Let her go!" he shouted. "I'll drop the traitor where she stands."

His words seemed to spark Rayna into directing her anger towards him rather than remain focused on K'lani. She turned on him seething with words pulled from the past. Even after a beautiful night together she wanted to hurt him.

"This isn't the first time you accused someone of being a traitor with no proof!"

"You're talking about the time I sent you away? I did that for your own good."

She gave a contrived laugh. "You accused me of the raid that killed Darius the Dreaded then called me a demon-eyed cyclops. That was for my own good?"

"No, that was the truth!" He almost spat his words. "That thing in your head looked demonic. You're better off having a hole in your face."

"I'll be better off shutting the hole in yours!"

The heat of words escalated until they came to blows. Such unbridled passion the night before turned sour with a singular event. Jagger tried to fight off his impulses of rage and hate but they grew too strong. Before he knew what happened, he struck Rayna across the cheek.

She tumbled into the dirt scrambling to fix the patch back over her eye. Jagger continued approaching intent on finishing the job. K'lani intervened using her makeshift spear with the dagger at the end. She swung it up over her back and then thrust towards Jagger's face. The tip came within inches of forcing him to need an eyepatch as well.

Ducking under another wild swing he caught the spear in a double-handed grip. Struggling to disarm K'lani he felt his balance give way beneath him. Both of them tumbled to the ground as Rayna swept their legs out from under.

The three of them continued to brawl on the ground. By now the fight drew the attention of the magic merchants. Many of them gathered around and began cheering on their favorites. To Jagger's surprise he heard most of them back K'lani. It made him want to strangle the life out of her.

He slithered over Rayna and went at K'lani's throat. As his hands snatched her a puff of smoke struck his face from above. The strange powder stung his eyes and throat. He rolled off K'lani and gagged trying to keep the mysterious substance from choking him to death.

~

Rayna watched as Jagger put his hands on K'lani's throat. Part of her wanted to watch him break her neck.

The other part thrilled at the thought of bashing his head in.

Before she could enact her plan Rayna saw Elden the magic merchant blow a foreign substance in Jagger's face. It caused him to flop around like a fish on land. Elden then blew the powder into K'lani's face as well. When he came for Rayna, she caught him by the wrists.

"Get away from me with that, old man!"

"Will help."

His words were clear but she still didn't understand what he meant. Having a strange substance blown at her from a magic maker wasn't something she would agree to. Pushing Elden back she grabbed K'lani's spear from the ground and lunged him.

Before she impaled the magic man on the end her companions stopped her. Each of them grabbed Rayna's arms and held her so that Elden could work his magic.

Rayna struggled and cursed. She tried to kick at Elden causing him to drop some of his magic powder. This made Jagger and K'lani force Rayna to her knees. They held fast as she pulled and seethed. Then the powder came. It drifted up her nose, into her open mouth, and even into the corner of her exposed eye.

A haze filled her head and she felt as though something sinister were being torn out. Rough coughs slammed her chest until a thick matter was expelled. She hacked up a few more bits of it and watched as the substance dissolved into the ground.

"What by all the gods was that?" Her throat was raw and her voice hoarse.

"Spell breaker," Elden told her.

Rayna stood on shaky legs. She took a swig off a waterskin K'lani offered her and spit upon the ground. Then she went after Elden. He tried to back away but Rayna caught him by the edge of his cloak.

"You put a spell on us?"

The man trembled in fear stuttering words Rayna didn't understand. She shook him and even went so far as to lift him in the air. His feet kicked out trying to find the surface while she yelled at him.

"Enough of these games! I just heard you speak our language."

"Stop it, Rayna," K'lani demanded. "He was trying to help us."

"He knows something," Rayna argued, lifting Elden higher still. "I'm going to find out what."

He struggled against her grip then finally gave in. "Followers of the chaos witch. Didn't want you here. They enchanted you during the night with dream dust. Quick to anger, paranoia. I fix, I fix!"

Elden started to cry then he urinated himself. Rayna set him down then turned her attention on the crowd surrounding them. Each magic merchant wore different color robes addressing their specialties. Rayna sought the amethyst robes. Dark and sinister colors set within a sea of simple greens, blues, and reds.

Her feet were swift and she caught one just as he tried to run away. With a fierce tug on the back of his robe she pulled the man back. Rayna yanked on his clothing so hard he left his feet and landed with a thud upon the ground. She stepped on his chest to keep him there then warned the rest of the magic users back.

"Where is she?" Rayna spoke through gritted teeth, the rise of her anger still prominent. "Where do I find the witch Nadiuska?"

Her captive began to laugh which caused her to increase the pressure of her foot on him. After a few constricted breaths he lamented and told her what he knew.

"Our queen is in the Majestic Mountains. But you'll never make it past all the defenses to reach her." The man grinned. "Even if you do get through she will kill you, dragon warrior."

Before Rayna had the pleasure of snapping the man's sternum he cracked a potion vile in his hands. The substance spilled out in plumes of purple smoke and suddenly the man disappeared from sight.

Rayna shouted in frustration and started towards her horse. She was intent on traveling day and night until reaching the Majestic Mountains. K'lani and Jagger were yelling at her to calm down, wait, and devise a plan with a clear head. None of that mattered.

All Rayna wanted to focus on was getting to Nadiuska. Let them face off on the witch's own grounds. She didn't care so long as an end came to one of them. But as she readied her horse she heard one voice calling out that stopped her.

"Rayna, help me!"

She had not heard the voice in so long she almost didn't recognize it. When she did match it to her fallen comrade it angered her. Storming back into the magic markets she sought Elden once more. This time K'lani stepped in her way to keep Rayna from assaulting the man.

"Who tricks me now, old man?" Rayna asked. "Why do I hear the voice of Valerios the Valiant calling to me for help?"

K'lani grew surprised and stepped back. She wanted answers from Elden as well. The magic man shook his head and spoke clearly.

"Not a trick. His spirit walks the Graven Peaks trapped between worlds."

The thought of Valerios stuck out on the frozen mountain all this time brought Rayna to tears. Her anger dissolved and she fell to her knees. It was her fault he followed the search party out that way. Valerios only accompanied them because Rayna asked him to.

Had she known it would mean his end she would've

approached things differently. If there was a chance to make matters right she needed to do it. Rayna owed Valerios that much after everything he gave up for her.

36
Dark Defender

Nadiuska basked in her new powers. An entire
army was at her whim. The Majestic
Mountains were fortified and the dragon
child sat in her dungeon awaiting its fate. It had taken
years to get to this point but Nadiuska accomplished
everything she set out to complete. The only matter left
to handle was the death of the so-called dragon warrior.

She underestimated Rayna's resolve to live. But as her
magic minion described his encounter with the one-eyed
woman and her companions, Nadiuska grew frustrated
with the girl's will.

The goblin-sized man appeared before Nadiuska as she
sat comfortably upon her newly carved throne. Hers was
fashioned from the blackest bark taken from the gnarled
trees of Mammoth Woods. To mark her glorious ascent

to god status it was embellished with fine silver.

"She was crazed, my queen," the sorcerer told her. "I'm lucky to have made it out alive."

"Yes, good of you to tell me. Now get him out of my sight."

Nadiuska motioned her guards. They hauled him away screaming. She didn't have time for spineless fools. The more urgent matter would be in locating Coraise Kennethgorian. His was a vessel she couldn't let get away.

She strode across the room to where Blahkbyrn was displayed vertically upon the wall. With everything falling into place her intent was to let the eye rest. But no sooner had she set it asleep upon the wall did she need its powers again.

"I'm sorry, my darling," she told the eye. "I shall have to call on you once more."

The jeweled eye of the dragon flashed open at the hilt allowing Nadiuska to see across the land. High and low she sought Coraise until finally locating him wandering aimlessly along the Dragon's Backbone.

Pinpointing his whereabouts gave her the opportunity to send her girls to fetch the mercenary. His mind, along with the rest of the Righteous Wardens, had been set under her power. But Coraise fought against her. Eventually she let him wander from the Majestic Mountains knowing she could herd her sheep when needed. Then Rayna returned and mucked it all up.

She sent the Daughters of Chaos to collect him and bring his dumb ass back to her. It didn't take them long to fetch him. Her daughters were endowed with great powers just like their mother. When they dragged him into the hall where Nadiuska awaited them he started to struggle against their grip.

"Come now, no need for all that." She set a hand upon his cheek to calm him. "You're home now."

"He seems to be fighting your connection to him, mother," Xara told her.

Nadiuska frowned. "A strong-willed warrior just like Rayna. I can't have that."

She twirled her sword in the air then set the tip against Coraise's chest. To Nadiuska's surprise, he pressed against it as though he welcomed death. The rebellious nature of the mercenary leader endeared him to her. She couldn't waste such talent.

"Leave us," she told her daughters.

They dumped Coraise to the ground but didn't go far. Each daughter went to a corner of the room and watched, ready to intervene if need be. Nadiuska wouldn't need them but she wanted them to see what true power looked like. It would give them something to strive for.

"I feel a rage deep down inside you, Coraise Kennethgorian," she said cupping his chin in her hand.

"You try to deny it but why? Embrace that side of yourself and you will be unconquerable!"

Nadiuska stepped back to the center of the floor with Coraise kneeling before her. With the snap of her fingers she retrieved an arcane staff. Amethyst runes carved into the wood grain marked an ancient energy only one with such power as Nadiuska could wield.

With a cross-hatch motion swung above Coraise's head she began to commune with a world few could pierce. Drawing from the eldritch power hidden behind the veil of darkness she began her spell.

Coraise began to seize upon the floor. Shivers racked his body as Nadiuska's incantations grew stronger. His limbs twisted and his skin split as she brought forth the thoughts that lingered at the deep recesses of his mind.

A bestial visage became prominent in his face first. His brow jutted out giving a monstrous appearance alongside deep set, black eyes. Black lips covered a mouth full of glistening yellow fangs. His body grew larger and more muscular than before with a greyish sheen of fear sprouting from his arms and legs.

Nadiuska stepped back and looked over her creation. She beckoned her daughters to come see as well. As the three of them stared at him, Coraise rose on his hinds quarters. He towered over the witches looking down with animalistic intent.

"You're beautiful," Nadiuska told him wiping tears

from her eyes. "A true warrior champion to represent my house. This bold berserker shall be Rayna's doom. Now go serve me well. Find the dragon girl and bring me her skull!"

The Coraise being gave a ferocious howl then stomped from the hall. Wants and needs from his human life washed away. He held a singular purpose now: scalp his defeated enemy and coat himself in her blood.

37
Lovers & Loose Ends

R ayna spent time away from the others trying to reconcile everything that occurred within the span of a day. Her emotions were jumbled with memories she felt detached from. Did she and the others go to blows off slights and insults? Had she truly made love with Jagger or was that too a trick of the mind?

She sat at the outskirts of Mako trying to make sense of it all. Her energy still felt volatile coupled with the grief of learning about Valerios. Whatever dream dust had been set upon them it hadn't fully been expelled from her yet. Never before had she felt so out of control, ready to split the skull of any who got in her way...her friends included.

When Elden came out to sit with her, Rayna wanted to tell him to run away. He wasn't safe around her. No one would be safe until she could calm down. Then, as if reading her mind, he handed across a pipe packed with ashwa...her ashwa.

She accepted the offer and enjoyed a few tokes. The herb washed over her mind and set it at ease. Rayna enjoyed one more puff then handed it back to Elden. Then she extended her hand to him.

"I'm sorry about before."

He nodded as though he understood and shook her hand in truce. Then he left her alone with her thoughts. She knew the longer it took her to reach Nadiuska the more peril Ryu was in. But she couldn't just leave Valerios' spirit trapped in this world. If not for his sacrifice it would've been Rayna's blood spilled on the Graven Peaks that day.

Her ruminating complete she sought her companions to tell them her decision. They were both in full armor, weapons at the ready with a few new ones tucked into their belts as well. Rayna approached with hesitance in case another brawl was about to break. But instead she found them ready to travel with her, whatever her choice may be.

"I must set Valerios free," she told them.

"Very well," Jagger replied. "We'll go with you."

Rayna shook her head. "It's too dangerous. The last time I climbed the peaks many deaths were felt."

"We don't have to climb. I can bring us to the top. The God of Wind is strong here. He will guide us."

So much of what K'lani said made Rayna uneasy. Not the least of which was her fear of heights which grew with every passing day. But she also held no faith in the God of Wind.

"Suppose halfway up your god looses interest and drops us?" she asked.

K'lani mistook her question for humor and insisted flying with her would be the safest means of travel. Jagger, intent on avoiding the Shadax who lived in the Shadowed Highlands, also agreed with K'lani's idea. Rayna's head wasn't quite fuzzy enough after indulging in the ashwa. But she saw limited choices if she wanted to stay alive long enough to get to Ryu.

"Alright, we'll do it your way."

Speaking the words didn't make Rayna fear the details of doing it any less. K'lani didn't waste any time readying herself either. She simply scooped up Rayna and Jagger in her arms and set off towards the Graven Peaks.

Rayna kept her eye shut tight the entire ride. But she could still feel her legs kicking wild in the air with no solid ground beneath her. Then she heard Jagger laughing. She opened her eye and found the source of his amusement was her.

"What's so funny?"

"I've never seen you scared before," he said. "It's cute."

Before Rayna could answer the three of them took a

tumble from the sky. It was just as she feared; the God of Wind let them think they were safe only to drop them to their death. But death didn't come. Instead, they hit the soft mounds of snow dotted across the top of the Graven Peaks.

"Sorry about the landing," K'lani told them. "I haven't learned how to control my abilities with the added weight."

It took a moment to acclimate to the thin air and cold surroundings. Once she had, Rayna felt a twinge of remorse pierce her heart. If only she could somehow go back and save Valerios from death. But no spell or god could turn back the wheel of time.

"What do we do now besides freezing to death?" Jagger asked.

"Elden said Valerios needs a proper burial," K'lani explained. "We need to find his body and lay him to rest in the way it is custom for his people."

As they discussed the specifics Rayna made her way over to the spot where her friend died that day. She steadied herself for what she would find there. His handsome features and lean body would be replaced by a gruesome sight. Rayna saw death more than most. She even witnessed loved ones pass right before her eyes. It never got any easier.

But as she walked closer Rayna realized no body remained on the mountain. There was also no sight of the massive dragon she'd slain, Saarath, Ryu's mother. She dropped to her knees and dug through patches of snow and dirt trying to find Valerios. With each clump revealing nothing Rayna started to panic.

"What is it?" Jagger said running to her side.

"He's gone!" she cried out, the sting of hot tears running over her face. "We can't set him free if Valerios' body isn't here."

K'lani and Jagger didn't know what to say to calm Rayna. They were only human, after all. The one who could put her at ease was no longer of this world. He came on a gust a wind, hovering over her as though he'd been there all the while.

"The body is simply a vessel for the spirit," the figure said. "I thought I taught you that."

Rayna sat back on her knees looking up at the hazy visage of her old friend Valerios. Had she seen a ghostly form other than his it may have frightened her right off the cliff side. But she knew even in whatever realm he was trapped that Valerios wouldn't harm her.

"You taught me a great many things. But what to do in case of your death wasn't brought up," she told him.

"It's simple really," Valerios said. "The spirit and the body come together to form one unique individual. Upon death of the body the spirit is severed and may lead a separate existence. This is not meant to be permanent. My spirit should not still be here."

Rayna stood trying to seek his eyes through the haze. "Tell me what I must do."

"I fear there's little you can do. Falkon brought my body to Saltwood Stronghold. Without my bones you cannot commence last rites."

"Then we'll return to Sandhal and retrieve your body." Rayna didn't care what obstacle she needed to overcome. Now that she was in his presence she was adamant about helping Valerios find his peace. Then Jagger reminded her of the other quest at hand.

"What about Ryu?" he asked. "If we veer off path back towards Sandhal it will cost us precious time. Coraise will have told the witch everything by then."

Rayna bowed her head uncertain of what to do for the first time in her life. She fought with the need to honor the vow to her dragon companion and with wanting to do right by her friend. Seeing her heart being torn in half, K'lani made an upstanding offer.

"I will go to Sandhal in your stead."

Rayna was at once relieved and concerned. "No, I can't ask you to do that for me."

"I'm not doing it for you," K'lani told her. "I am honoring my sister by laying to rest the man she was meant to marry."

"Sweet K'lani," Valerios voice was a whisper on the air. "Tell Kemi I am sorry for not meeting her as I promised."

Knowing the matter was settled Rayna felt a great swell of relief. She hugged K'lani tight around the neck and thanked her. Then she turned back to Valerios to see her friend one last time.

"I'm sorry for everything."

"I'm not," he told her. "I got to meet the legendary dragonslayer and learn that she was much more than any tale could ever tell."

"But had you not stood up for me you'd still live."

"I died with honor. Don't let your guilt rob me of that."

Valerios turned to K'lani. "I would travel with you to Sandhal but alas my spirit is trapped within the Shadowed Highlands."

"I'll be quick," she replied.

"Farewell, Rayna," Valerios called to her before fading out from view.

Rayna had so much more to say to him but her emotions choked off her words. Only fits of tears came with a great want to embrace Valerios once again. Instead, she turned to Jagger and let him hold her until her sobbing faded.

K'lani brought her companions back down to the town of Mako. Then the three of them split up for their separate quests vowing to meet again in Theopilous when all was completed. While K'lani headed south towards Sandhal, Jagger and Rayna turned their attention east to the Majestic Mountains.

38
Berserker

T he journey towards the witch's stronghold was arduous stretching from the Shadowed Highlands deep into the farmlands. For the long leg of it Jagger and Rayna spoke few words. Only when they came again to Josep's farmhouse did the conversation pickup. Still, they only spoke on the necessities and nothing deeper.

They were surprised to see the farm still remained unoccupied and in good standing. Perhaps being far off the public path is how Josep and his family survived so long. Without knowing it was there the farmhouse was hard to spot. Thieves such as Jagger would travel past it towards more open areas searching for targets.

He let Rayna soak in a bath while he found something to cook up for a meal. She needed time by herself to explore everything that occurred recently and the emotions that went with it. Rayna was a hard ass by nature. She wouldn't let herself feel easily, especially not when others were around. Jagger gave her the space to grieve her friend Valerios.

He needed some time alone to ponder as well. Such dedication Rayna felt for this dead man that she would throw away her mission to do right by him. Seeing the woman she'd become in their years apart made Jagger regretful. Had she been at his side all this time perhaps he would've become a better man as well.

"No time like the present," he said aloud.

To his surprise, Rayna responded. "No time for what?"

Taken off guard by her presence Jagger scrambled for a cover-up answer. Turning with a large bowl of fresh stew in hand he used the meal for a distraction.

"No time like the present to eat."

He ladled out the stew into individual bowls placed upon the kitchen table. Rayna filled their glasses with water they'd collected at Watersnake River and then boiled for purification. Jagger kept his head down while eating trying to come up with a way to breach a sensitive topic. Rayna beat him to it.

"You don't have to go any further," she told him. "In fact, it's better if you stay here while I travel on ahead."

He stopped eating and leaned back in his chair to look at her square in the face. Her one beautiful blue eye met his stare and did not falter. The request, or more likely demand, aggravated Jagger.

"Stay here and do what? Become a farmhand?"

"Don't get upset."

"I'm not upset. I want to know why you're pushing me away."

"It's not that. I just think it's safer if you remain here."

"You don't get it do you?" He leaned forwards and placed his hand upon hers. "I'm not going to let you charge off into the mouth of madness on your own."

Rayna pulled her hand away and stood. "You don't owe me anything, Jagger. Stop trying to make up for the past."

He stood as well and circled the table to block her exit from the room. Taking her hands once more he let himself fall into the words he'd been wanting to say since they found each other again.

"I'm not talking about the past, I'm thinking of our future...together. I love you, Rayna. I always have."

Before she withdrew, before she spoke, Jagger pulled her to him and kissed her. Rayna resisted for a moment then met him halfway. With their passion building, Jagger lifted her into his arms and walked the stairs to the first bedroom he could find.

The bed was small but coupled together it would hold them both easily. Jagger let his love for her pour out; his body speaking deeper than a thousand words ever could. But in the morning, Rayna had gone.

~

Rayna never felt so close to anyone as she did Jagger. Their bond went back to a time of youthful innocence that grew deeper with time. Even in the distance that separated them she never stopped loving him either. But because Jagger held Rayna's heart she couldn't let him follow her into certain death. To this end, she left him as he slept and set off on her own.

Riding during the early morning hours she traveled in darkness. A brief storm of lightning, thunder, and wind passed over with vengeance then dispersed as suddenly as it started.

The sun didn't peek its head up over the mountains until she reached the edge of Mammoth Woods. As the warmth of sunlight carried down across the valley Rayna saw someone awaiting her there.

Deep inside the woods he stood almost rivaling the height of the trees. She could not make out his face nor gauge his posture. From the look of him it appeared as though man met beast. Rayna's thoughts carried to Damaris de Paz and the last time she walked Mammoth Woods.

Night Howlers attacked her then. Each of them the size of a man but built like a wolf. Now this new creature presented itself to her. The beasts lurking inside are why many avoided going through Mammoth Woods altogether. Rayna didn't have the time to go around. She would meet this creature head on.

Slipping from her horse, Rayna dipped into the saddle bag and procured a dragon-horned helm to protect herself further. Before leaving Mako, the magic merchant Elden fashioned it as a gift for her. Crafted to match her body armor, it remained lightweight and allowed Rayna to keep her vision unobstructed. An important element to have when fighting with only one eye.

She let the horse go on its way intent on finding it again after the battle. But as Rayna stepped closer to the beast in the woods a familiarity crept over her. The creature's gray-black lips pulled back to reveal yellow fangs as it spoke.

"I've come for your head."

The creature's voice was guttural but still recognizable as that of Coraise Kennethgorian. Rayna looked over the unnatural length of his limbs and the grayish fur sprouting from them. His once handsome face now a grotesque mask with hollow, dark eyes.

"What has Nadiuska done to you, Coraise?"

"Berserker," he replied.

"You were a man, a warrior named Coraise Kennethgorian and lead the Righteous Wardens," Rayna explained. "This isn't you. I know magic makers that can help. Let me try and help you."

The mercenary leader of the Righteous Wardens may have been swayed with that type of deal. But this

Berserker wouldn't be bargained with. He knew only to follow the orders of his queen. That meant tearing Rayna limb from limb. With no fear of death, he went into a trance-like fury and bounded towards her.

~

Jagger dressed fast as he could and rushed out the door. In his haste he almost forgot to grab his weapons. Horse half-saddled he returned to the house to grab his axe and a short sword he bought from the magic makers.

He spent quite a bit of coin before leaving Mako but it was worth it. To see Rayna's eyes light up at the reveal of her new helmet he would've spent all he had. Jagger insisted to Elden that his part in the gift be kept quiet. All he wanted was to see her smile again. Now he wanted to keep her stubborn head from being lopped off her shoulders.

Pushing his steed as hard as it would ride, Jagger set out on the path he knew Rayna would've taken. Following Watersnake River up and then into Mammoth Woods she would go.

He ran into her once before deep inside the Fickle Forest. If she'd been brave enough to traverse those woods nothing would keep her out of Mammoth. He only hoped he could catch up with her before she found herself in trouble.

~

Rayna prepared for the Berserker's charge but not his strength. Even a glancing blow sent her body spinning through the air. She landed hard on small stones lining the ground. Using any trick she could think of she took those same stones and threw them at the Berserker. It wouldn't inflict any damage but it would distract him long enough for her to rebound.

Coraise was already the most skilled opponent Rayna ever faced. Now he was the strongest and most dangerous as well. He turned his face to block the stones from striking his snout. This allowed Rayna to get to her feet. She took out the bone whip and lashed it out towards the Berserker's throat. He lifted a brawny arm and caught the length of the whip around his forearm.

Rayna pulled with both hands trying to gain some advantage. The Berserker proved too strong. Pulling her forward she fell on her stomach knocking the wind out of her. With her body prone the Berserker produced a sword from a sheath at his back.

With the strength and size of him the beast didn't need a weapon. Now that he was armed it made him even more deadly. Rayna had to keep on the move to avoid being split in half by the large blade. She rolled across the ground as the Berserker slashed down at her.

One near miss almost took off her head. She got to her feet and took hold of her whip again praying she could keep him at bay with well-placed strikes. But he was able to shrug off even the most excessive punishment the whip put out.

Another swing of the Berserker's sword caught Rayna in the helmet. It staggered her off balance but she kept her head. Thankful for the reinforced protection the helmet gave her Rayna stopped playing coy with the Berserker.

"You're getting tired, Coraise, I can tell." she mocked. "This is the longest battle you've ever been in."

He grunted and howled almost tearing at his own face. Then he softened. His sword arm lowered and he begged her.

"Kill me."

He spoke as Coraise not the Berserker. His human side took control once more to beg for the sweet release of death. Having been controlled like a puppet her entire life Rayna knew his pain. Though Coraise was the reason Ryu had been taken she would not wish him to suffer at the hand's of Nadiuska. Rayna would gladly give him his wish.

A close range arrow shot came whistling through the trees. It struck the Berserker high upon the shoulder grazing his flesh. He shrugged it off; the attack proving only to enrage him. When Rayna sought the archer she found Jagger riding towards her. She tried to wave him off but he continued charging the beast.

The Berserker gave out a howl that shook the trees. He hefted his sword ready to chop Jagger in half as he came closer. Running off emotion, Rayna disregarded any rational sense and ran for the Berserker.

He spotted her coming and swung towards her. Using the elements in her favor Rayna bounded up the thick trunk of a tree to avoid the blow. The Berserker's sword embedded in the wood causing it to get stuck there.

As Jagger rode by he tossed Rayna his sword then continued on to distract the Berserker. The beast left his own blade stuck in the tree intent on ripping Jagger in half with his bare hands. He wouldn't get that chance.

Rayna used her bone whip to lash around the Berserker's feet causing him to tumble to the ground. With his height advantage broken, and struggling to get to his feet, Rayna leaped atop him. Sword outstretched she used all her bodyweight behind the strike as she landed.

The blade cut him clean through the neck causing blood vessels to burst. He bucked and writhed in pain knocking Rayna off his back. Stumbling backwards the Berserker fell into his own sword catching himself in the side.

He hung from the tree like a piece of meat strung up for sale in the markets. With Jagger racing to her side Rayna readied herself for a continuing battle. Instead, the Berserker looked towards her and smiled. His dark eyes softened and he slipped away into death.

"By the gods if I didn't love you already I would surely love you now." Jagger embraced her with such fervor she almost fell over.

Rayna wanted to chastise him for coming after her. In her head she carried the many reasons it was better for her to go alone to the Majestic Mountains. But after surviving certain death at the hands of the Berserker beast she could think of only one thing to say.

"I love you too."

39
Dragon's Lair

They stayed the night in the town of Turk which rested at the base of the Majestic Mountains. There they replenished their strength, made love, and acquired new weaponry including climbing gear before setting out on the morrow.

The next day, fearful of what may happen when they reached the witch, Rayna and Jagger decided to solidify their expressions of love with keepsakes. Marriage ceremonies were a fools game. But they wanted something to represent their new beginning before it ended.

A local inker marked designs on their forearms. Using a small sharp bone and wooden mallet he inked two circular bands: one thin and one thicker to represent the two of them together. The process stung the skin. Where they were headed it would be the least of the pain they faced.

High into the mountains they rode without a single stop along the way. Too much time had passed since Ryu was stolen from Rayna. Now would be her moment of revenge for everything the witch Nadiuska put her through. First, they would have to cross the threshold inside her mountain of power to face her.

As they drew closer the air felt thicker on each inhalation. Now Rayna understood what K'lani meant when she sensed the growing darkness upon the world. Rayna wished the Ischon girl were at her side knowing the magic powers that awaited them. Two against many would have to do.

When it felt as though they couldn't climb any further the fortress revealed itself. Carved deep into the cliffs of the Majestic Mountains stood a massive dark castle. The only way to differentiate the rock from the castle itself were the plumes of purpura smoke wafting out from windows. Arcane magic swirled on the air giving off an illumination that almost welcomed the invaders.

"She knows we're here," Rayna said. "No sense trying to be subtle."

Reaching across her horse she kissed Jagger full on the lips. They pressed their foreheads against one another then readied for battle. Alongside the bone whip resting on her hip, Rayna had purchased a hand-forged sword.

Expertly produced by the master craftsmen of Turk, the

sword had an elaborate guard and pommel with a 38-inch blade tempered for strength. Jagger maintained his own sword crafted by the skilled hands of Elden in Mako. It wasn't ideal going against dark magic and the powerful Blahkbyrn blade but it would have to do.

The entryway into the witch's domicile looked like a gaping mouth. From this pit a wave of soldiers suddenly began charging towards Jagger and Rayna. They ran in single formation across a bridge fashioned from black rock.

The two warriors centered themselves and then spurred their horses to meet the attack head-on. If they let the soldiers come at them en masse it would cause them to get surrounded and slaughtered. Their only hope was to charge through the defensive line on the narrowing bridge.

Weapons in one hand, holding fast to the horse's reins in the other, Rayna went hard at the first wave. She cleaved and cut a path through the former Saltwood Soldiers. Jagger took up the rear dispatching any whom Rayna let slip by.

They used the horses to trample more soldiers or ease them over the side of the bridge into oblivion. The tactic was working until they reached the main gate. There at the threshold the Daughters of Chaos awaited them.

Dark and light, night and day, they contrasted each other but were equally as powerful. Jagger and Rayna knew firsthand that the daughters wouldn't be an easy fight. So, they decided not to fight them at all.

They rushed the gate where the daughters awaited them. Spurring the horses hard and fast the two warriors stood in the saddle continuing forwards. The daughters stood their ground ready to engage their foes as they approached. At the last second both Rayna and Jagger dove up over their heads.

The Daughters of Chaos watched them somersault through the air completely forgetting about the horses. As Rayna and Jagger landed inside the castle the horses trampled over the daughters. Relieved their plan had worked they continued with the next part of it.

Using their swords they cut free the chains securing the main gate. With nothing to hold it in place the iron bars slammed into the ground effectively keeping the remaining horde of soldiers outside. Pleased with the success of their ideas it was now time to find Ryu and Nadiuska.

"I think we need to split up."

Rayna's suggestion was met with a look of concern and then panic from Jagger. Before she could question his intentions he was throwing Rayna to the ground. Her body collapsed in a heap knocking the dragon-horned helmet from atop her head. When she looked up a sting of fear gripped her heart. The Daughters of Chaos lived and they held Jagger aloft by his neck.

40
Daughters of Chaos

Instinct always served Rayna well. When she was the mighty dragonslayer it was instinct more than anything that drove her to greatness. Even with the witch Nadiuska in her head, Rayna relied upon that part of herself that reacted with certainty.

That type of engagement with her enemies is what always kept her safe. She followed her instincts again in the entry of the dark queen's castle to keep her lover alive. Using the whip at her side she lashed it out, not towards either of the daughters, but at Jagger.

The whip wrapped around his waist securely and as it did Rayna pulled with all her strength. Such erratic movement caused her to fall backwards on her rear. But when she looked up she was relieved to see Jagger pulled free from Xara's grip.

He tumbled across the floor to Rayna's side. The two of them stood together, back-to-back, ready to battle the

Daughters of Chaos. It took Jagger a moment to shake off the crushing grip on his throat. Once he found his voice again he employed one of his own tactics that got him through tough times. Jagger was the master of deceit.

"Now is your chance. Kill your sister!" He called out ambiguously to confused the daughters into thinking the other was their ally.

The convincing nature of his lies always made the target question their own existence. In this case, Xara fell prey to his trap and accused her own flesh and blood of betrayal.

"You would defy me? Defy mother?"

Her accusatory tone caught Xiamara off guard. Hands flexing with the need to unleash Chaos Magic on someone she turned from the warriors and to Xara instead.

"Are you a fool such as Falkon Fourspire?" Xiamara asked. "So easily swayed with words to do the bidding of a human?!"

The comparison to a man she kept as a puppet for over a year wounded Xara. She shrieked until the walls rumbled at her tone. Xiamara grew disgusted with her lighter half but did not engage in a physical altercation. Breaking their blood bond wouldn't be easy. It didn't need to be. All Jagger intended was a distraction long enough to gain the advantage. With Xiamara's back to them it was now Rayna's turn to do what she did best.

With a running leap she dove towards Xiamara and plunged her sword in between the woman's shoulder blades. The force of the blow caused the tip of the sword to burst out of Xiamara's chest. Her blood spattered across Xara's face as she watched with stunned horror.

Death of a Chaos Daughter proved unsettling to all. They did not go quietly nor clean. In her throes of death Xiamara thrashed wild around the room causing Rayna to be flung into the far wall. Her sword remained embedded in the woman's torso while she writhed upon the floor.

Xara tried to help her sister only to find her body turn to a pile of gelatinous blood in her hands. She tried to scoop up the remnants of Xiamara and hold her sister close as she wept. With Xara distracted, Jagger moved in for the kill.

Rayna remained dazed in the far corner of the room. She watched Jagger move too swift towards the remaining daughter. Xara heard him coming before he could strike. Incensed with a need to avenge her sister, Xara's attack was more ruthless than before.

She began blasting streams of fire from her fingertips towards Jagger. His arms became singed as he blocked his face from the attack. Xara pressed him back against the opposite wall where he curled himself into a ball to try and absorb the flames. He wouldn't survive long.

Rayna dashed over to the remains of Xiamara to collect

her sword before making her way to the others. Xara was toying with Jagger by lashing his body with small marks made of flame. They cut through his leathers and burned his flesh. Each time Xara struck Jagger's screams grew louder until he begged for the mercy of death.

Xara relished in his misery. His pleas for the end would go unanswered as he continued to unleash punishment upon him. But she didn't know he played a game of wits with her. In Jagger's time with the Forsaken Force he learned to absorb pain. The longer Xara drew out his death the greater the chance of Rayna reaching them in time.

Sure enough, as Xara's focus remained on torturing Jagger, Rayna came up on her side. With a double grip on her sword she swung hard and fast to cut the witch's arms off at the elbows. The chaos magic ceased giving Jagger the respite he needed to survive.

Xara looked upon her bloody stumps and began screaming. She turned towards Rayna trying to engage a spell. With another hard swing Rayna took her head off before the magic could be completed. It rolled up towards Jagger who kicked it away in disgust.

Rayna came to his side. Burns covered his back and arms causing him to shake in pain. She took her cloak from off her shoulders and wrapped him in it. He forced a smile at her.

"How's my face?"

"Beautiful as ever." She kissed his forehead then held him against her bosom. "Rest here. I'll continue on."

"No, Rayna, it's too dangerous."

She rose and sheathed her sword. "I must find Ryu."

"Then I'll come with you."

Jagger tried to get up only to collapse back down against the wall. As much as he wanted to help the pain was too severe. Rayna couldn't be worrying about him while trying to track Ryu. Jagger finally understood that. He tucked himself in a corner while Rayna sought the witch Nadiuska on her own.

41
Dark Dragon

T he witch's dark castle was vast. Rayna could spend days searching and never find where she tucked Ryu away. So, instead of aimlessly walking about she sought her dragon from within.

When she came to a crossroads inside the castle she knelt down and spoke aloud.

"Ryu, where are you?"

From the moment he stepped free from his egg and into her hands the two of them shared a bond. If Nadiuska could seek her through the dragoneye jewel across all those years then Rayna could tap into her bond with Ryu the same.

The castle split in three directions. She could go back the way she came, continue forwards up a great granite staircase, or head down within the bowels of it all. Rayna sought the answer from within and as she did she heard the faintest of cries echoing from below.

Tucked away from the light like a prisoner of war Ryu

awaited his fate. Whatever Nadiuska had in mind for
him wasn't going to happen now. Rayna would see to it
that Ryu escaped even if it cost her own life.

Sword drawn she headed down into the bowels. There
were no windows that deep underground. Only
torchlight upon the walls allowed Rayna any sense of
direction. She removed one from its sconce and
continued deeper still.

As she went further down into the depths Ryu's cries
grew louder. Knowing he was so close made Rayna
move faster even in the dimly lit corridor. Her long
journey finally came to a close as she found Ryu chained
up like a dog. In her haste to free him Rayna didn't check
the corners for safety first. She was struck in the side of
the head which knocked her to the floor.

Falling on her hands and knees her first instinct was to
wave the torch at her assailant. As she turned towards
the attacker the fire chased away the shadows and
revealed a face in the dark. Nadiuska herself smiled back
at Rayna.

~

Nadiuska knew the dragon warrior would come
running when she heard the little one cry out. A few
pokes and prods on Ryu the dragon and he began to
throw a fit. At the same time, Nadiuska heard her
Daughters of Chaos crying out. A part of her wanted to

go to them but she knew that would be a mistake. Better to stick to the plan and lull Rayna into her trap. Xara and Xiamara's deaths would be vindicated with the fall of the dragon warrior.

~

A trap. Rayna should've been ready for it but her emotions ran too deep. Concern for Ryu blinded her to Nadiuska's truly devious nature. Using the torch as a weapon Rayna lunged at her hoping to set fire to her wicked face. Nadiuska batted it aside and knocked Rayna back. The blow was infused with magic and sent Rayna spilling.

"I had such high hopes for you," Nadiuska said, slipping her heavy cloak from her shoulders. "But now I've come to realize you're just a foolish whelp of a girl and I'm going to enjoy killing you."

Nadiuska had no intention of fighting woman to witch. Instead, she summoned all the arcane energy from the depths of darkness into her own being. Rayna watched in terror as Nadiuska's body twisted and turned; her form expanding from woman to weapon.

Her size grew immensely pushing against the rock walls and tearing up through the floorboards until she breached the entire back of the castle. Leathery wings sprouted from her back and a massive tail formed from her spine.

Rayna looked upon the snout and rows of sharpened teeth in both dismay and disgust. There it was before her, the one she sought for so long to avenge her family. Nadiuska had become the dark dragon.

The sight of her enraged Rayna and she made another foolish mistake. Charging headlong towards the dragon with her sword extended she narrowly missed being burned alive. Except Rayna studied dragons for over half her life. She knew when the beasts set to expel their fiery breath.

On the last moment she dove out of the way to come up behind the dragon. Slashing at its hind quarters with the sword Rayna quickly realized the blade held no effect. It bounced off the hardened scales and snapped in two equal halves.

Undaunted, Rayna continued to strike with the broken blade. This caused Nadiuska to lash out with her long tail. The bony protrusions struck Rayna on the hip and knocked her off balance. Her stagger-step gave the dragon an opening. The massive maw reached down and snapped at Rayna catching her around the waist.

If not for Valerios' armor fitted to her body, Rayna would've been skewered by the dragon's teeth. But she still remained in danger of being crushed by the jaws. Tucking her arm inside the mouth she grabbed her whip and lashed it to a nearby sconce.

The dragon fought against her for a moment then spat

the warrior free. Rayna landed hard on the floor causing Ryu to react with concern. She caught his eyes upon hers and noted him motion with his snout.

Rayna followed his direction and saw a familiar piece of her history set within the folds of Nadiuska's cloak. Blahkbyrn the witch had called it but Rayna always knew her sword by another name. Her greatsword Bhrytbyrn had never let her down in a battle against a dragon. Today would be no different.

Rayna lunged over and grasped the sword by the hilt. The dark dragon seemed to laugh at her as she stood with the blade in front of her. It reared back with plumes of smoke rising from its nostrils ready to ignite the entire room.

Rather than try and kill the dragon Rayna used Bhrytbyrn to release one. She swung the blade around and snapped the chains holding Ryu by the neck. No longer constricted by his bonds the red dragon let his own fire fly.

His flames were small but sure of aim as Ryu targeted Nadiuska's face. The dark dragon hissed and growled from the attack. She tried to back away only to run into a load bearing pillar. Large stones broke free and fell atop her head causing her to droop. That is when Rayna made her final move.

Without the dragoneye embedded in her skull she couldn't call flame to blade. Instead, she set the sword within Ryu's stream of fire to ignite it. With Bhrytbyrn alight in her hands once again Rayna sent the blade to Nadiuska's heart. Beating beneath the scales sat the darkened soul of the one who made her a killer. It was only fitting that the last dragon Rayna slayed was the dragon queen.

42
Dragon Rider

Only after the dark dragon had fallen did Rayna come to realize the extent of her wounds. One of the long teeth had punctured through her armor and caught her deep in the side. She cupped her hand over it trying to keep blood from spilling out.

Ryu noted her pain and tried to comfort her with small licks of his tongue. He was not without his own wounds having been at the mercy of the witch for so long. But his concern lay with Rayna rather than himself.

He nosed at her injury and then pushed his body beneath hers. With her consciousness slipping from lack of blood Rayna let herself fall upon the dragon. She expected him to walk her out towards Jagger and the main gate where they would make their next move. Instead, Ryu spread his wings and lifted up.

Injured or not her fear of heights brought Rayna awake.

Before she could slip off Ryu's back he was already high in the air. She clung to his neck as he moved higher into the sky. Soon Rayna felt comfortable enough to ease herself sitting and allow Ryu to lead the way.

Looking back at the crumbled ruins of the queen's castle Rayna hoped Jagger found his way out before the fall. Knowing the dark witch Nadiuska lay dead gave her a sense of peace as she felt a life-long quest come to an end.

But within the embers of the fiery corpse of the dark dragon Rayna sensed source magic stirring. She felt one weight lifted only to be replaced by another just as frightening.

But that is another story....

END OF VOLUME II

I hope you enjoyed *Rayna the Dragon Warrior* as much as I enjoyed writing it. Please leave a review at your favorite online retailer.

Reviews help authors maintain momentum with our writing by letting us know which types of stories are resonating. Plus, writing is a very isolating career and I really enjoy hearing feedback from readers!

A Time of Dragons continues....

Special Excerpt
Rayna the Dragon Rider
A Time of Dragons III

Copyright © 2024 Cynthia Vespia

Ryu carried Rayna on his back for miles before his energy gave out. He started a downward spiral somewhere over the ocean. In Rayna's weakened condition all she could do was cling to the dragon as they spun out.

Fortunately, Ryu managed one last push to keep them in the air. They came close enough to the water that his tail trailed across it. The cool splash across her skin roused Rayna enough so she could help steer Ryu towards land.

He jutted up across an expanse of desert that made Rayna believe they were back at the Red Waste. But as he flew deeper across the island she realized he'd brought them all the way to Kartha.

Memories of her time there came back to her in a flash. Some good; mostly bad. Rayna tried to get Ryu to turn around and take them back to Atharia. She needed to find Jagger and K'lani. Promises were made to reunite at Theopilous after the war with the dragon queen ended. Rayna intended on keeping that promise.

RAYNA   DRAGON WARRIOR

Ryu would have none of it. He was weary from flying and the long time spent in captivity. Once they found themselves over land he didn't hesitate to touch down. Flying on the back of a dragon with a fear of heights is not something Rayna would ever get used to. When he landed, she rolled off his back and retched on the ground.

Once Rayna composed herself she took a look around. Ryu set them down in an obscure area of the island near the beach. If she could find a boat large enough to hold a dragon it could get them back to Atharia before her past deeds in Kartha caught up to her.

Find out what happens in

Rayna the Dragon Rider
A Time of Dragons
Volume III

Appendix

Names:
Rayna (Rain-ah)
Bhrytbyrn (bright-burn)
Blahkbyrn (black-burn)
Nadiuska (Nad-e-ooh-ska)
K'lani (Kay Lan E)
Saarath (Sar-rath)
Damaris de Paz (Dah-mare-is-dee-paz)
Xiamara (Zee-ah-mara)
Xara (Zar-ah)
Valerios (Val-air-e-ous)
Favian (Fay-vee-an)
Falkon (Falcon)
Atharia (Ah-thar-e-ya)
Pelanor Pass (Pel-ay-nor)
Ischon across the Sea (E-shawn)
Emperor Kivu Kazu (Kee-Voo Kah-zoo)
Theopilous (Thee-op-ilous)
Valeuki (Val-ooh-kai)
Coraise Kennethgorian (Core-ace Kenneth-gore-ian)
D'zdario Dizdar (Diz-dar-e-o Diz-dar)

About the Author

"Original Cyn" Cynthia Vespia writes fantasy novels with bite including urban fantasy vigilantes and heroic adventure fantasy. Her books have featured a secret group of superhero renegades; the dark side of vigilante justice in Las Vegas; and a duo of demon hunters fighting supernatural beings. Her latest venture is an exciting adventure series about a dragonslayer who has a change of heart.

Cyn received a "Best Series" nomination for her fantasy trilogy Demon Hunter. Her novel Karma ranked #1 on Amazon twice in several distinct categories including superhero, action-adventure, and contemporary fantasy. She has been published in anthologies such as Skelos Press and Dark Eclipse.

Her characters are outcasts and anti-heroes with depth

and real vulnerabilities. Each novel plot is designed to give heroes a challenge and villains a purpose. The worlds Cyn creates are a gritty mix of fantasy, magic, and the supernatural while exploring the theme of "success through struggle." She's expanded this theme into personal development books and guides.

Cyn has also written content for Microsoft, UFC, WWE, HBO, Netflix, and more. As a former fitness competitor she enjoys keep active through training. Cynthia is available for conventions, interviews and workshops.

Sign up for the newsletter and receive the Time of Dragons prequel Rise of the Dragonslayer for free
https://www.cynthiavespia.com/free-story

Follow on Bookbub:
https://www.bookbub.com/authors/cynthia-vespia

Follow on Facebook:
https://www.facebook.com/originalcynwrites

Follow on Instagram: @originalcynwrites

Follow on Youtube:
https://www.youtube.com/c/OriginalCynContent

Books by Cynthia Vespia

SILKES STRIKE FORCE
(superhero urban fantasy)

Karma

Kobra

Kaged

Khaos

VEGAS VIGILANTES
(dark urban fantasy)

Casino Empire

Lucky Sevens

Vegas Valkyrie

Sin City Assassin

DEMON HUNTERS
(heroic adventure fantasy)

Demon Hunter Saga

Demon Huntress Legends

OTHER BOOKS

The Crescent

Theater of Pain

Sins and Virtues

NONFICTION

Be Your Own Superhero

Made in the USA
Columbia, SC
10 March 2024

32430474R00183